SKULKY DUANE

By

Guy Shackle

For

Finn Koemtzopoulos

Chapter 1

The red Parcel Force van pulled up outside the old thatched cottage. Despite the mazy country lanes, the Satnav had worked perfectly. Jim the driver jumped out whistling. He carried a square box about two feet in diameter. It was wrapped in brown paper and sported a foreign postmark. He knocked on the door and waited impatiently. It was opened by Belinda Porter in her dressing gown.

It was early and the first delivery of the day. She signed for it half asleep and carried the parcel into the kitchen. It was addressed to her husband who was in the shower. Taking a pair of scissors from a drawer, she cut through the paper and lifting the lid, peered inside. Her piercing scream brought him scurrying downstairs with his towel round his waist. He found his wife sprawled on a chair. Her eyes were glazed and her mouth open. On the table, staring out of its box, was a human skull. Its protruding forehead and deep eye sockets set off a row of handsome yellow teeth. These were fixed in an unnerving grin.

"Goodness me," gasped the half naked figure. "It's Duane."

He shut his eyes to picture the friend he had not seen for over ten years. He'd never known his African name. He was a labourer on the oil platform where Keith worked as an engineer. The Englishman spent five years in Nigeria before retiring to North Devon aged sixty. He was a tall man with a shock of white hair and a bleached complexion from his long sojourn in the tropics. The pair had become acquainted when Duane fished the engineer out of the sea after his safety harness snapped. The hapless victim had gone under twice before the huge black hands pulled him clear.

The large amount of water he'd swallowed was forced out of him with practiced ease. The sodden figure was voluble with his thanks and later had a chance to repay his debt. His rescuer's nephew was badly burnt stealing fuel from a leaking pipe that caught fire. Keith took him to hospital and paid for his treatment. The best surgeon in Lagos was hired and he went on to make a good recovery.

This brought invitations to visit Duane's family. He and his wife lived in a shack on the edge of a pineapple grove. On the engineer's first visit, Lola had prepared an enormous feast. The table overflowed with every kind of delicacy. And with it came a vast jug of local wine. It was the start of a warm friendship. Keith became a regular visitor, bringing tit bits from England and bottles of duty free whisky.

The pair would sit on the porch in two wicker chairs sipping steadily. The late afternoon would turn to dusk and then night. The moon was high by the time the guest made his unsteady way back to his living quarters on the rig. Their talk often become philosophical, full of long silences as each considered their replies. Silent that is, of human voices. The din of croaking of frogs was all around.

One night Keith brought a two litre bottle instead of the normal one. Yet its contents slid down as easily as all the others. Their conversation became ever more profound. And their deep friendship became deeper. Clutching his glass tightly, Duane spoke with emotion. "Keith, we must always be together."

Yet he knew in truth, they were worlds apart. The engineer had a wife in England while his roots were deep in his own soil. But what of the next world? Could they be united there? The speaker was convinced they could. If they were buried together. Nobody knew what happened when you left this life. But the closer you were in death the better the chance.

Many people have hoped for this before Duane. But Keith was not one of them. Being an engineer, he was a practical sort. Once you were gone, that was it. There was no other existence. But the whisky was coursing through his veins so why upset a friend? Why ruin a blissful evening getting wonderfully drunk under the stars? And of course, it would never happen. He would retire to England and they would lose touch. Neither were letter writers.

So when Duane gripped his shoulders in a tearful embrace, he agreed. Yes, in the same grave. He privately thought it would be a squeeze with Belinda in there too. But it would never happen, and he would never tell her. Yet emotions ran high as the two hunched figures pledged eternal loyalty with clinking glasses.

But the commitment for Keith faded the following morning. As it would anyone fighting a crushing hangover. And soon he forgot all about it. Duane too, never mentioned the subject again.

As the engineer predicted, they did go on to lose touch. When he retired there was a poignant farewell with promises of eternal friendship. But nobody mentioned a grave.

He came out of his reverie. Belinda sat opposite him in a state of shock. He wanted to explain what had happened, but she was in no condition to listen. He would let her come back to her senses first. He peered into the box. An envelope was tucked in the bottom. Gingerly he lifted it clear of the skull. Using a blade of the scissors, he carefully slit it open. Inside was a letter from Lola explaining she was honouring her husband's last wish. But only part of it. She could not afford to send the whole skeleton. Money was tight so the head would have to do. It should be enough to reunite them in the next world. She also apologised for sending it second class. Duane would have been upset, but luckily wouldn't know. He had died after being hit in the street by a speeding car. It had been a wonderful funeral. Everybody in the village had attended. She had waited for the ants and worms to do their work. Then one night she crept to the grave and dug up her husband. With one swift blow of her meat cleaver, she had removed the head and reburied the rest.

Keith felt Belinda stir. He fetched her a glass of water and watched her sip it. Then taking her hands in his, he told her the whole story. And then read her the letter. When he had finished she looked at him aghast. She couldn't take in what she had heard. The whole thing was absurd. Yet it couldn't be. There was the skull looking at her on the table. It seemed to be saying 'now we are three.' She shook her head violently to get rid of the thought. It was all nonsense. But what were they to do with it?

It was a question exercising Keith's mind. His first idea was to bury it in the garden. It would be a good storage place. He had no intention of dying for a long time yet. But what would happen when he did? He quickly quashed the thought. It had just been a drunken evening. A promise made on the spur of the moment. Nothing in writing. Well, not until the letter. But there was no contract. So was he responsible?

Belinda broke into his thoughts. "It's a disgusting object. We must get rid of it."

"I agree. I'll dig a hole for it near the hedge. We'll plant a rose bush on top. Duane will like that."

"No, we can't have it hanging around. We'll go for a drive and toss it out somewhere."

Keith suddenly found himself feeling protective. "We can't do that. I made a promise."

"You didn't mean it. It was just an inebriated conversation."

"He meant it. I feel I can't let him down."

"You're not really suggesting putting it in our grave when we go? What about me? I don't want somebody else's skull in there with us."

"I didn't say that. I just think we ought to keep it handy but out of sight."

"But Duane won't know anything about it."

"We can't be sure. These African societies have potent spells."

"Surely you don't believe that? This is ridiculous."

"I don't want to take any chances."

"I can see you've spent too long out there."

"We won't make any hasty decisions. I'm going down to the pub to think about it."

"Well don't leave that thing here with me. Take it with you. Put it in the boot."

"I don't think Duane would like that."

"He'll hardly fit in the glove box will he? And you can't leave him on the passenger seat. He'll terrify anybody looking in the window."

"Don't worry. I'll put my coat over him."

Chapter 2

It was only a five minute drive past open fields. Keith spent it talking to Duane. It just seemed natural. After all, they had been the closest of friends. He said not to worry about Belinda. She didn't dislike him. It was just his unexpected arrival had been a terrible shock. She would soon get over it. Then she would treat him as part of the family. He pulled into the White Hart's car park. It was a traditional country inn with low beams, white walls, and endless brass fittings. It was opening time and he was the first customer.

Reggie Bartlett, the landlord, greeted him with surprise. He was a florid, rather overweight figure with receding sandy coloured hair. "You're early today Keith. Been chucked out have you?"

The visitor pulled up a stool. "Belinda's had rather a shock, so I thought I'd disappear for a while." He felt for his wallet. "A scotch and soda please." He watched the glass being pressed against the optic. "I've had a surprise package delivered today."

The publican nodded sympathetically. "I never like surprises. Bad for the nerves."

"You can say that again. This one shattered Belinda's and didn't do much for mine." Keith paused. His first instinct was to keep the whole thing secret. It was so macabre, it would be daft to publicise it.

Yet like many others in such situations, he had to tell somebody. And Reggie turned out to be an avid listener. The publican said not a word until the speaker had finished. Then there was a moment of astounded silence. Finally he said. "I've heard a few stories standing here, but that's amazing. If you didn't say you had it in the car I wouldn't believe you."

Keith took the hint. "You want to have a look?"

Reggie lifted the bar flap. "Come on then, there's nobody else here." He followed the skull's new owner out to the vehicle. The engineer opened the passenger door and removed his coat. The head, caught by the sun's rays streaming through the window, appeared to sparkle.

Keith felt a sharp intake of breath over his shoulder. "So that's him," muttered his companion. "That's your African mate."

"Well part of him."

"How come you never told anybody about your promise?"

"To tell you the truth, I forgot I'd made it. I was dead drunk at the time and Duane never mentioned it afterwards." He replaced the coat and they returned to the bar to find old Sid Comfrey waiting. The engineer was about to ask the landlord to keep his secret but he was too late.

"Keith's got a skull in the car," he declared. "He's going to be buried with it."

The newcomer had difficulty taking this in. He was not fast in word or deed. He spent his life trailing a few yards behind his wife. Especially out shopping. The only exception was when they approached the pub. Then he would push his way to the front. But Joyce wasn't with him. Being Tuesday, she was having her hair done. Later he had to repeat to her what he'd heard, syllable by syllable. He opened his packet of crisps "What's he doing with a skull?"

"It's his friend. They're going into the same grave so they can be in the next world together."

He popped one in his mouth. "You're having me on."

"It's an amazing story," said the landlord. He turned to the engineer. "Can I tell it this time? To see if I've got it right?"

Keith found himself giving a hopeless nod. By nightfall the whole village would know. He extracted himself and slipped out of the door followed by Sid's curious gaze. Back home munching bread and cheese, he told Brenda what had happened. She looked thoughtful as she buttered another slice. "Do you think broadcasting it was wise? The whole thing is bizarre and I find it most unnerving."

"I couldn't help myself. I had to get off my chest."

"But you know what the villagers are like. First they'll gossip about it and then they'll want to see it."

"Reggie already has. And he's told that Sid Comfrey."

"Well there you are. And that's only the start."

"You're right. The best thing is for us to take up that invitation from my sister. We'll go away for a couple of days. Let things die down a little."

"Don't forget my mother is coming to clean tomorrow. She'll have a heart attack if she sees that skull."

"We'll take it with us."

"Oh no we won't."

"Ok. We'll put it in its box in the garage. It'll be safe there."

The pair let the subject drop. They did not want it to spoil their break. And it was certainly not one to discuss with relatives. Yet it continued to lurk at the back of their minds as they took advantage of his sister's riding stable to potter around the country lanes on horseback.

They returned to find a terse note pinned to the kitchen's notice board. It was from Belinda's mother. She did not mind spring cleaning, but objected strongly to finding sickening mementoes from her son-in-law's travels. The skull had been thrown out. Keith frowned as he read it. "What was she doing in the garage?"

"You know she pries everywhere."

"Well, it's out of our hands now. The rubbish was collected this morning."

"Yes, it must be fate. At least you've got a clear conscience. It was not your doing."

He brightened. "You're right, it was an accident."

It was as if a heavy weight had been lifted. The atmosphere in the cottage became carefree. The couple were starting a jolly dinner that evening when the phone rang. It was Belinda's father on the line. "Your mother's been rushed to hospital in a coma," he said in an agitated voice. "She started babbling about a skull and collapsed."

The couple were at her bedside within the hour. Only one thing had been on their minds as their car sped through the darkening countryside. Neither could bring themselves to believe it, but was Duane to blame? Surely it had to be a coincidence? But then why did she talk about him? The doctor they saw was baffled. The victim was strong and healthy and early tests gave no hint of the cause.

There was no point in sitting beside the comatose figure. They would be alerted if there was any change. They motored home in silence. Keith was in no doubt they would have to find the skull. Otherwise his mother-in-law could die. But how much time did they have? And would they ever find it? It looked an impossible task. The local tip was huge and that's where it would be. But what could they say they were after? It could hardly be a human head. No, they would be searching for a lost family heirloom. A necklace or a brooch. He pictured the pair of them scrabbling around in a mountain of refuse. It would be hopeless. He turned to his wife. "We'll never find it on our own. What we need is an army."

"Where are you going to find one?"

"In the village."

"Do you really think anyone's going to volunteer to hunt for a skull in that stinking heap?"

"I am sure they will. They are a nosey lot, and have nothing else to do."

"I can think of better ways to combat boredom."

"Well, I can only ask." He reached for the phone. "Reggie can be the recruiting officer. He'll know who's likely to take the plunge." Keith briefly explained the mission and that time was of the essence. They would have to be at the tip when it opened first thing in the morning. There was an audible intake of breath at the other end. Followed by silence.

"Reggie are you there?"

"I'm here Keith, and I'll be there tomorrow. I don't know if anybody else will."

"Please, it's important."

"I'll try one or two and see how we get on. The trouble is, I don't think anybody will want to touch it after what's happened to your mother-in-law."

"All they have to do is help find it. I'll do the handling."

"All right. But don't count on too many." An hour later the landlord rang back. "You're not going to believe this Keith but I've got twenty. The whole village is backing you."

The engineer gasped with relief and poured out his gratitude. Then telling Belinda the good news he escorted her up to bed. They would need all the rest they could get.

Chapter 3

The sky was just becoming light when the couple pulled into the pub car park. They had arrived to lead the convoy on the two mile journey to the tip. There were eight people waiting to board the pub's mini bus. Reggie detached himself from the group. "I'm afraid there's been a few withdrawals. I asked some at closing time. They've obviously sobered up."

"Don't worry," replied Keith. "It looks like we've got enough."

The motley crew were sensibly clad in their oldest clothes. Andre, the young White Hart's chef, was already getting on everybody's nerves. He was chubby with thick dark hair and an annoying habit of sucking his teeth. But nobody could fault his popular shepherd's pie. Sid was there too, having bits of fluff picked off his faded jersey by Joyce. And so was the Reverend Pottie. He had thought long and hard before volunteering as a grave had been desecrated. But Duane had sounded a decent fellow and the motive for removing his head understandable. And he felt he had to help a parishioner. Even if Keith was not often seen among his congregation. The vicar of St Peter's was gangling with more hair on his eyebrows than his head. These waggled when his sermons became dramatic.

The other couple who had got up early were Rita and Tom Joint. They were the sort of pensioners who had to be doing something. They prepared a daily list. The first job should have been cleaning out the goldfish pond. Followed by a walk to the dry cleaner's with Tom's tie. But these were swiftly superseded when the call for volunteers came. As Tom said, groups all over England would be setting out on different projects. Yet it was safe to say no others would be hunting for a skull on a rubbish tip. The pair at least would have plenty of energy for the task. They kept themselves fit and both had trim figures with a bounce in their step.

The search party was completed by Trish Trumpet. Trish the Dish as she was once known, had left that complimentary label far behind. A blonde divorcee in her sixties, she would play her part but had an entirely different reason for joining up. She was not concerned if finding Duane would bring Keith's mother-in-law out of a coma. Oh no, it was saving Basil the young orphan seagull she had raised. It fed at the tip where the council was organising a cull and she wanted to discover what was happening.

The volunteers excitedly boarded the mini bus and the small convoy set out. The gates were opening as they arrived. The caretaker, a squat man in a yellow jacket, eyed the visitors. He scratched his ear as they disembarked. "We don't normally get tourists."

Keith opened his mouth to reply, but Trish's voice was already filling the air. "I demand you stop the shooting."

"Ah, you've come about the seagulls have you? Well it's no good protesting here. You'll have to go to the town hall."

Trish's voice rose an octave. "I refuse to let my pet be killed."

The official had no intention of getting involved in an argument, but could not help himself. "They can't identify each bird before they fire can they?"

The engineer with growing impatience, stepped between them. "We're not tourists or protestors," he declared. "We're a search party. A valuable piece of jewellery has mistakenly been thrown out. Can we hunt for it?"

His listener looked doubtful. It was against the rules

for unauthorised persons to gain admittance. Health and Safety and all that. But he was a reasonable man. They could have a look until the lorries started arriving. That was in four hours. He didn't want anybody to be buried under tons of refuse. At this, there were several vigorous nods of agreement. Keith stated his address and the date of collection and a nearby mound was pointed to. As the party approached it, a most pungent aroma greeted their nostrils. The engineer leading the way, vowed to apologise to Duane if they found him. It made sense after what happened to his mother-in-law.

Belinda broke into his thoughts. "I hope the head was put in the right bin."

"Of course it was," he replied. "You wouldn't recycle a skull would you? It's bound to be here"

The party spread out. Joyce waved Sid forward. He shuffled in her direction wrinkling his nose. The vicar quickly got stuck in. An enthusiastic fisherman, he wished he'd worn waders instead of gumboots. There were excited cries when anything suspicious was spotted. But sadly there were only false alarms before the first lorry arrived. The official rushed up to shoo the searchers away. "That's your lot. You can try again tomorrow if you want." He pushed his cap back on his head. "You wouldn't believe it. We found a skull yesterday. A big one with great yellow teeth."

Keith heard his voice coming from somewhere else. "Really, what did you do with it?"

"Took it to the police station of course. Obviously a murder victim. Killers like doing that. Leaving pieces all over the place. Mind you, it didn't look too battered. Just a small dent at the back."

Keith sucked in his breath. So it was Duane. He'd once mentioned a coconut hitting him there as a child. His mother had said it was his own fault for playing under a tree when it was windy. He used to finger the dent nostalgically when drunk, remembering his young days.

The engineer felt it was not the time to tell his companions they'd been on a wild goose chase. Fortunately they were already heading for the mini bus with determined strides. Promising to stand them all a drink in the pub, he and Belinda hurriedly took their leave. The police station was six miles away in the next village. Gripping the wheel tightly, Keith hurtled through the narrow winding lanes.

"Slow down for goodness sake," begged Belinda. "Or we'll have a crash."

"Every second counts," came the terse reply. "If we lose track of Duane I don't give much for your mother's chances."

"Don't be ridiculous. I've told you a thousand times, the whole thing is pure coincidence."

"Maybe it is, maybe it isn't."

At last they arrived at their destination. Keith quickly parked and strode ahead of his wife to the front desk. His request brought the constable to his feet. He summoned the senior sergeant who looked at them darkly. "You'd better come in here," he said, leading them to an interview room. He pointed to two chairs in front of an empty table. He seated himself behind it as they gingerly took theirs. The officer surveyed them grimly. "Now could you say again why you have come here."

"It's about my friend's head," replied Keith and went on to tell his extraordinary story.

His listener was unmoved. "A fanciful tale" he said, leaning forward. "Ok, which one of you did it?"

Keith looked perplexed. "Did what?"

"Murdered the victim." Receiving no reply from his

astonished companions, he went on. "Whichever one of you did it, you've done the right thing. It's always better to give yourself up than wait to be caught. It's so much easier on the nerves." He reached for his pad. "Now I'll take your initial confessions."

"No, it's not like that at all," declared the engineer as Belinda turned deathly pale. He spelled out again exactly how the skull had come into their possession. It was a long time since sergeant Hopps had had his hands on real live criminals, and he was reluctant to believe in their innocence. Keith drew out his wallet and carefully extracted Lola's letter. "This will back up my story."

He handed it over to his interrogator who peered at it with distaste. "It could be a clever forgery. You know, covering your tracks."

The engineer just managed to stifle a sigh of frustration. "Do you really think I would make up a cock and bull story like that? I know it's far fetched, but it happens to be true."

The sergeant raised his eyebrows. "And this skull has magical powers that put your mother-in-law in a coma?"

"I don't know. But it's a worrying co-incidence. It's one I don't want to take a chance with. That's why I want it back quickly."

"I'm afraid that's not possible."

Keith looked perplexed. "Why?"

"It's not here."

"Not here?"

"No, it's gone to the laboratory in Bristol for forensic tests. To see if it matches the details of any missing persons or murder victims. We find quite a few decapitated bodies."

The engineer put a hand to his brow. "How long

will all this take?"

"It depends on how many tests have to be made and the priority the skull is given. It's a very busy place."

"Can't you hurry it up?"

"What reason do I give? To bring a woman out of a coma? They'd laugh themselves silly and I'd be taken to a psychiatric ward."

"Well, can't you think of something?"

"I'll do what I can, but I shall want your names and address. I shall have to make a report about this and you may well be needed for an interview."

"All right," said Keith with exasperation and gave their details.

Belinda spoke for the first time. "You do believe us sergeant don't you?"

"In truth madam, I don't know what I think. It's not every day I get someone coming in asking for their friend's skull back. Especially one that's meant to have knocked out your mother. But I have to say you look a respectable couple." He paused for a moment. "Mind you, there's plenty of your sort that commit murder." He stood up. "Anyway I'll give you a ring as soon as I hear anything."

He watched them depart with a shake of his head. It certainly was a rum situation. He'd never come across anything like it during twenty five years in the force. How could a skull put a spell on anybody? Yet he would do his best to help. If he didn't, it might put a spell on him. He laughed to himself, but it was a short one and had a nervous edge.

Chapter 4

Keith and Belinda drove slowly home. On the way they called at the hospital. There was no change in the patient's condition. That evening the engineer bought his promised round in the pub. He confessed their search had been a waste of time. He should have revealed to the official what they were looking for. He expected an angry reaction but instead received plenty of sympathy. Everybody admitted they would have done exactly the same. They would not have wanted it known they were hunting for a skull. It just didn't seem right. Not in a respectable English village.

But what had the sergeant said? They crowded round as he explained where the head was and his plea for its quick return. This brought sombre nods of agreement. Whether you believed it had dark powers or not, it was better to get it home. And having been part of the search, the onlookers were feeling protective about it.

So the next forty eight hours were a time of nail biting. Not only for Keith and Belinda, but for the whole village. Even for those not involved, it was the major topic of conversation. It was exerting a strange fascination. The phone in the cottage kept ringing. Each time Keith snatched it up hoping to hear the sergeant's voice. But it was only a local desperate for news. In the end he had to ask for the line to be kept clear.

When the call came it was not from officer Hopps. It was detective inspector Clive Howard. He would be returning the skull and would have a few questions to ask. If that was all right. Keith wondered what would happen if it wasn't, but hastily agreed. The speaker would be arriving the following morning at ten. Well timed for coffee and biscuits. Belinda hurried off to buy the best ones the corner shop had to offer.

Dead on time a squad car crunched up the gravel drive. An angular man with slightly stooped shoulders emerged. He pushed a lock of black hair into place and looked carefully around him. Then reaching across to the passenger seat, he took out a cardboard box and headed for the cottage. The engineer and his wife, watching through the lounge window, felt a flood of relief. The officer could only be carrying one thing. Duane was coming home. The front door opened before the approaching figure could put a finger on the bell.

"Good morning inspector," said Keith. His visitor looked surprised. He had half expected to find a hippy camp or a bizarre religious cult. Instead he was looking at the very picture of a down to earth middle class couple. Belinda shepherded him into the lounge while Keith hurried to the kitchen to open the box. He let out a heartfelt sigh. Yes, it really was Duane. The yellow teeth smiled at him reassuringly. He had feared a mix up at the laboratory. Whatever the tests carried out, the skull looked undamaged. He didn't like the idea of his friend being prodded about.

The inspector first apologised for keeping the head for so long. It was not that their explanation was disbelieved. It had to be eliminated from other investigations. Keith agreed this was necessary. But now it had been, what further did the officer want?

His listener gave a slight cough. A final check. Just for the record. To tidy everything up. "We need the widow's details," he explained. "So we can ask our Nigerian counterparts to get her to verify your story. We've seen her letter which appears perfectly adequate, but there is nothing like hearing it in person."

Keith could not hide his dismay.

The officer's voice betrayed a note of surprise. "You

object?"

"No, it's not that. It's just a very delicate subject. None of her family or friends know. She did not want to cause unrest in her village. That's why she did it in the dead of night. Police making inquiries could cause quite an upheaval. In fact, there could be hell to pay."

"Do not worry. We will ask for it to be done with the utmost discretion. A meeting will be arranged away from prying eyes. You know, a few quiet words. Just confirmation."

The engineer still looked unhappy. "I really hope you will stress that. I know the country well. They are an outgoing people. Not ones for a few quiet words."

Belinda arrived with a laden tray. "Is everything sorted out?"

"Yes," replied her husband. "Well almost. The police want to check the Nigerian side of it."

"All a matter of routine," asserted the inspector. "I'm sure we won't be troubling you again. You'll just receive a quick call to let you know when the matter is completed." He reached for a biscuit. "But I must say it's been my oddest case. I've come across all sorts of blood brother pacts but nothing to compare with this." He turned to Keith. "You must have been fond of the fellow."

"I was. He saved my life."

"It's a big commitment you made."

"It was just one of those things. A moonlit tropical night and a gallon of whisky."

"Ah yes, alcohol can help you make outlandish decisions."

"It didn't seem outlandish. I was serious at the time as you are when you're drinking. But deep down I never thought anything would come of it. Neither of us referred to it again."

"So it must have been a big shock when the skull arrived."

"It certainly was. Belinda nearly died of fright."

"What? She opened it?"

"Yes, I was in the shower. I've never come down stairs faster."

The detective pulled at his fingers. "So what do you think about this coma business?"

"Obviously pure co-incidence, but the timing was uncanny. And the doctors have yet to find a medical reason for her condition. That's the extraordinary thing."

"And the most worrying," added his wife.

"You never know what to read into these things," replied their visitor. "You have to have facts to go with your imagination. That's one thing I've learnt in this job." He rose to his feet. "Well, I'll be off. I wouldn't worry about it too much if I were you. I am sure it will work out all right in the end."

The pair watched his car execute a neat three point turn in the drive and disappear. As they did so, the phone rang. Belinda picked it up. She listened intently and her face suddenly cleared. "It's the hospital," she blurted out. "Mother has come out of her coma."

Keith clutched the back of a chair. "When?"

"About forty minutes ago."

He looked at the clock on the wall. "That's almost exactly to the moment when the inspector arrived."

"Or to be more accurate," ventured his wife. "When Duane did."

"Yes," he replied, staring at her. "When Duane did."

Chapter 5

The news that Keith's mother-in-law quickly recovered when the skull was returned, gripped the village. It spread from lip to lip like wildfire. The engineer said it was like sending up a flare. Belinda was upset that well wishers were more interested in seeing Duane's head than the patient.

In the end, the couple bowed to the inevitable. There would have to be a meeting. They could hardly make a grand tour with it stuck on top of a pole as Andre suggested. So instead of taking it to meet the people, they would bring them to it. They would host an early evening drinks party where Duane would be displayed. At first they intended just inviting the searchers. But such was the interest, they had to make it open house. Better that, said Keith, than having to deal with gatecrashers.

Much thought was given to where to station the prize exhibit. It must be visible from all angles without being close enough to touch. Not that anybody would dare to do so after what happened to Belinda's mother. Her daughter caught herself worrying that Duane might dislike being ogled at. She felt he was beginning to spook her. Her unperturbed husband said his friend would love the attention. He had always been the life and soul of a party. She was about to point out it was only his head, but thought better of it.

Finally it was decided to put the skull on the dining room table surrounded by snacks. When helping themselves to these, guests could look at it surreptitiously rather than be seen deliberately staring. This was important because Duane, as both Keith and Belinda agreed, had a particular way of looking back at you.

Trish was the first to arrive which Keith thought showed nerve. Especially as she had been more interested in saving her seagull than joining the hunt. She said she hoped he didn't mind, but she had threatened a council officer with the skull if he didn't call off the shoot. The engineer said he did mind. He minded very much indeed. Duane's skull was his property and nobody else was allowed to use it.

"So what was the official's reaction?" he demanded.

"He said I was mad," she replied. "He then led me gently from the room."

Keith's anger subsided at this happy ending, but it was worrying. The skull was generating enough unhealthy interest locally without it spreading further afield. The room began to fill up. Soon there was unseemly jostling. Those reaching the edge of the table, with its unrivalled view, were reluctant to make way for newcomers. These tried to push their way in with their elbows. Others stood on tiptoe to see over the crowd. It was an uncivilised scrum. And for one thing, disrespectful to Duane.

Standing on a chair, Keith called for everybody's attention. His friend was to all effect, lying in state. So would those wishing to see him, file past from left to right. This immediately restored order. Surveying the scene from his elevated position, the engineer felt Lenin in his Red Square mausoleum would have been proud of the decorum. Even moving slowly, it was impossible to take in every detail, so many guests went round several times. Keith was generous with his drinks and the atmosphere became increasingly jovial. The sedately moving queue gradually began to resemble a conga. The watcher did not mind. As he had said, Duane enjoyed a party. The skull looked to be appearing more cheerful. Or was it the gins the

25

engineer was knocking back? He'd had a few more than usual. But he refused to blame himself. He'd needed them. And so did Belinda. She was faithfully matching him glass for glass.

He felt a presence at his elbow. It was Reggie. The landlord exuded a rather superior air. Having been the first to inspect the skull in what was a private viewing, he could afford to keep himself above the crush.

"Quite a party, Keith," he remarked. "Speaking as a professional in the entertainments trade, I think it's an excellent show. They've all had a good look with plenty of drink to help them do it."

This was true. If nobody was actually scared of the exhibit, they didn't want to attract its attention. So they were resorting to sly glances rather than staring it out. One or two, drunker than the rest, were bravely giving it a leer. But only a very short one. Everyone kept a respectful distance. That was until Hilda Strict came to leave. Grey haired and plump, she was a colourful character. She had received a suspended prison sentence for fraud at the age of seventy five. She popped her husband in the freezer when he died and drew his pension for six months before being discovered. The local undertaker was suspected of tipping off the authorities, being angry at the loss of business.

She couldn't decide whether to drink white wine or red, so had several glasses of both. This made her think of her Fred. He must have been lonely in his ice box. What a pity Duane had not arrived earlier. He could have been stored in there to keep him company. She had to rely on her stick to keep herself upright. But as she headed for the door, she turned and deftly raising it, leant across the table and prodded what might have been her husband's companion. "You behave yourself," she cried.

The end had a rubber tip so no harm was done. Although Duane did slide backwards a few inches. There were gasps of horror and then a deadly hush. The onlookers on either side of the attacker parted as if the Red Sea. They were terrified of being associated with her. She, oblivious of their concern, went merrily on her way. The vicar, realising she should be escorted home, plucked up his courage to hurry to her side. Taking her by the arm he led her out onto the drive. Yet despite his holding her firmly, she somehow slipped from his grasp and crashed to the ground. Her piteous cry split the air and she began sobbing. With the help of Keith, he carefully carried her back inside.

Her left ankle was already ballooning. X-rays would show it was broken. A silent and subdued crowd watched her being loaded into the ambulance. As its tail lights vanished into the darkness, a babble of voices broke out. Nobody had wanted to utter their thoughts in Hilda's presence. Now their fears surfaced. Duane had done it. He'd toppled her for poking him. There could be no other explanation.

Yes there could, pleaded the engineer. It was pure co-incidence and could be rationally arrived at. Mrs Strict was drunk and could hardly stand up. Even when sober she was unsteady on her feet. That's why she had a stick. But what about the vicar? they cried. He had a good hold of her and had said so himself.

"Yes I did," admitted her escort. "She just seemed to slip away from me. It was most strange."

"Of course it was," intervened Andre. "I saw Duane wince when she poked him."

"Don't be so stupid," replied Keith angrily. "It's only a skull."

"It definitely changed its expression," retorted the

chef defiantly.

"What did it look like?" asked Sid who had edged forward despite himself. "Was it one of those 'I'll get you for that'?"

"No, it was more like a cheerful wink. He was saying 'you just watch this.'"

Keith held up his hands. "We've all had enough for tonight. It's time to go home now."

And nobody needed urging. Despite the brave faces, the widow's fate had shaken his guests more than they cared to admit. It was noticeable that as each left, they said goodnight to the skull. Or at least nodded respectfully in its direction. As the door closed on the last departure, the engineer sank onto the sofa. His wife was already there. She looked at him with glassy eyes. "That head has got to go." Her voice betrayed a mixture of drink and nerves but was demanding nevertheless.

Keith looked over his shoulder. "Sssh, he'll hear you."

"God, you're as bad as the rest. He can't anyway, he's in the next room."

"I agree something must be done, but we can't make a hasty decision. At least the circus is now over. There's just Mrs Watson left."

"Are you sure letting her see it is wise?"

"Well, her daughter seems to think so. She said the old girl was upset at not being able to come this evening. But at ninety five and partly bedridden, you could hardly expect her to. So if she can't come to us, we'll go to her. It's unfair for her to miss out when everybody else has had a peek."

"But she can't be far off becoming like Duane herself. It could be unnerving knowing that's what you'll soon look like. It's like very ill people attending funerals."

28

"It won't apply to her because I've heard she's going to be cremated."

"If only Duane had been," came the heartfelt reply.

"Well, it's too late for that now."

Keith intended to pop in with it only for a few moments. It would not do to give the old girl nightmares. It was decided the visit would take place at eleven o'clock in the morning. That was when Mrs Watson was usually at her brightest.

As the hour approached, she told her daughter she felt like a little girl at Christmas. She was positively twitching with excitement underneath the bedclothes when the front door bell rang. Keith waited nervously on the doorstep of the red roofed bungalow with its neat flowerbeds. Lodged in his brain was Belinda's last minute warning. A nasty shock could kill a person of her age. He was not a magician pulling a rabbit out of a hat. He must produce the skull slowly and carefully from its box. The engineer had kept the one it had arrived in. It would make Duane feel more at home. He carried it in a shopping bag. His wife had rummaged through her collection to find the most impressive. Unfortunately the Harrods one was torn, so it had to be John Lewis.

Audrey ushered him in. "Mother is waiting for you. She hasn't slept much but is as bright as a button."

Her visitor hesitated. "It's not too late to change your mind."

"No. She would never forgive me if I stopped you now."

"It can be quite a unnerving sight."

"You've seen most things when you're ninety five."

The engineer felt he had made his point and would have a clear conscience if the worst came to the worst. Whatever that might be. But as he entered her room, there was no cowing under the bed clothes. Mrs Watson was sitting bolt upright with her hands clasped before her. "Bring him out," she cried. "Bring him out."

So without further ado, Keith delved into the bag and produced the box. He felt her gaze fixed on him as he opened the lid and lifted Duane into the sunlight. It showed him off to his best effect and Belinda had given him a polish. The widow put her head on one side. "What a pretty boy," she exclaimed. "He must have been very handsome with his skin on."

"He was," the engineer agreed. He had not expected such an enthusiastic welcome. But what happened next, took him aback. Mrs Watson put out a hand. "Let me chuck him under the chin. I know he'd like that."

"Are you sure you want to?"

"Of course I'm sure. He doesn't get enough affection."

He edged up the side of the bed and placed the skull before her. Her ancient fingers stretched out and tickled Duane gently. "Coochie, coochie, coo," she said brightly. "Coochie, coochie, coo." The exertion was too much, and her hand fell back on the counterpane. Keith carefully removed the skull and went to put it back in its box.

"No, no, not yet," came the anxious voice from the pillow. "We've only just met."

"Your daughter said I mustn't tire you out."

"Tire me out? I haven't had such an interesting visitor for ages."

"That doesn't say much for the rest of us."

"No offence, but it's true." She continued to stare at the head with half closed eyes. "Do they clean their teeth in Nigeria? His are quite yellow aren't they?"

Keith was desperate not to get involved in what could be a dangerous conversation. "I don't think he would like you mentioning that would he?"

"Probably not, but they could do with a good brush. Mind you, so could a lot of people's these days."

Audrey appeared in the doorway. "How are we getting on?"

"Very well," replied the animated figure. "Duane's quite a character isn't he?"

"He's just a skull after all, mother."

"Yes, but he's got something about him."

"I can't say I know him well enough."

"You don't have to know him. You can just feel it. He brightens the room." She looked at the engineer. "Isn't that right Mr Porter?"

"Well, Duane's certainly impressed you. I'm so glad you've had a chance to see him."

"So am I. Audrey does her best for me, but I get so little entertainment."

"Too much can be just as bad for you," replied her daughter. "I really think it's time for the skull to be put away. Mr Porter will have other things to do."

The widow sighed. "If he must. But I'm very grateful I've had the opportunity to be introduced to Duane. I can see why the whole village is talking about him."

Keith seized his chance to remove the exhibit from her admiring gaze. And at the same time turned down the offer of a cup of tea. He did not want to be rude, but was keen to escape. There had been some strange reactions to the skull, but Mrs Watson's was the most bizarre. He wondered if she was becoming a little soft in the head. Yet Audrey assured him on the way out her mother was quite sane.

"Who's a pretty boy then?" he muttered to the box as he walked the short journey home. What a caper! Duane was forming his own fan club. Belinda was waiting for him at the door. "Audrey's already been on the phone," she exclaimed. "Her mother was so thrilled by your visit, she's decided not to be cremated after all. She's going to be buried. Apparently bones are much more attractive than a pile of ashes."

But how long before that happened? That was what Keith was thinking. She had said Duane's teeth were dirty. Would he would punish her like he had his mother-in-law and Mrs Strict? He grimaced. The skull was getting to him. As it was everybody else. Of course it was only a piece of bone. It had been forensically tested hadn't it? It must have been manhandled in the laboratory. Yet nothing had happened to the police scientists. As far as he knew anyway.

But where should Duane be kept? They could no longer bury him in the garden. A lot had happened since that first day when it seemed the best idea. No, he would be more comfortable in the house. Keith pulled himself up short. He was at it again. Giving the skull human feelings.

Belinda suggested the lounge window. It would go well with the yellow curtains. The engineer said that wouldn't do. Everybody would peer over the hedge when they passed. Especially Andre. He was the sort who pulled faces and waved. In the end Duane was put on top of the bookcase in the hall. Up there, they would not need to look him in the eye.

Chapter 6

Three days later Belinda answered the door to two men. They wore sombre suits and each carried a clipboard. "Harry Smith," said the tallest who had a rather pinched face. "This is my colleague Norman Abbot."

She stared at them blankly.

"Environmental Health," said the smaller one, who had shiny swept back black hair. "We've come about the skull." Belinda's eyes widened, but she said nothing. She was trying to take their visit in. As was Keith who appeared at her shoulder.

"We've heard it is a danger to the public," explained Mr Smith. "That's what they're saying."

"That's what who's saying?" asked the engineer.

"We've had a complaint."

His listener's brow wrinkled. "You've had a complaint?"

"Yes."

"Who made it?"

"I'm not at liberty to divulge."

"What is it then?"

Mr Abbot cleared his throat and glanced at the sheet in front of him. The pair reminded Belinda of a double act taking it in turn to read the news on television.

"Well, to keep it brief. It's accused of putting Mrs Sorrell in a coma and breaking Mrs Strict's ankle."

"Anything else?" asked Keith, trying to keep the rising anger out of his voice.

"Yes," replied Mr Smith. "The hand of the technician carrying out the forensic tests has been crushed. A colleague accidentally slammed a door on it."

"Exactly," retorted Belinda, "accidental is the word."

"The pair have worked together for twenty years and nothing like that has ever happened before."

"There's always a first time for everything." replied Keith.

"Yes, there is," answered Mr Abbot. "This is the first time we've had to investigate a skull and I have to say it mystifies us."

"You're joining a select club which is collecting new members every day."

Mr Smith squared his shoulders. "Can we see it?"

"Yes you can," replied the engineer. "But I'm telling you, it's just a piece of bone."

The pair were ushered inside.

"Where did you get it?" asked Mr Abbot.

"Come and have a cup of coffee first," said Keith. "I will tell you how it happened."

He settled his visitors on the sofa while Belinda busied herself in the kitchen. They heard him out in silence. Afterwards they scratched their heads and trailed into the hall. Standing on a chair, Keith gingerly lifted Duane down.

"It looks pretty lifeless to me," admitted Mr Smith.

"Of course it is," replied the engineer irritably. "It's the top part of a skeleton."

"I can see that," came the huffy response. "But it's got a reputation for doing evil things."

"But is that justified?" asked Belinda. "There is a rational explanation for everything that's happened."

"That's as maybe," sniffed Mr Abbot. "But we've got to file a report."

"What are you going to say?" asked Keith.

"That's the trouble, it's a bizarre case."

"Well whatever you write, you'd better be careful."

Mr Smith frowned. "What do you mean?"

"Of course it's all in people's minds, but if the skull

does cast spells, it punishes anybody who upsets it."

"What are you getting at?" said Mr Abbot.

"If you cast aspirations on its character, it may become angry. It could be dangerous for you even to drive home."

The officials said nothing but looked at each other. Mr Smith rubbed his ear pensively. "We can only report what we see."

"Exactly. And now you've seen it. A piece of harmless bone." Keith put it back. "Who sent you on this wild goose chase anyway?"

"We have to look into every complaint. The public's safety is paramount."

"Ah yes, that complaint. You really can't tell us who made it?"

"Sorry, we can't divulge anybody's identity."

"Whoever it was should be reprimanded for wasting your time," declared Belinda. "You'd think people would have something better to do."

"I hope you're not referring to us," said Mr Abbot.

"No, she's not," said her husband disarmingly. "We know you have your regulations." He saw no point in upsetting such an officious pair. They had come, they had viewed, and they'd heard the story. The skull would stay on top of the bookcase where it could do no harm. As far as he and Belinda were concerned, they could write whatever they liked. They could make themselves look foolish if they wanted to.

The visitors were ready to leave. They promised their hosts they would be sent a copy of the report. Keith said he would look forward to it. It should make interesting reading. Still gripping their clipboards, the guardians of public safety returned to their car. Mr Smith was the driver. Mr Abbot advised him to take it easy. "We don't want a speeding ticket. Not after where we've just been."

Chapter 7

The police report from Nigeria and the one from Health and Safety arrived on the same day. And their verdicts were as expected. The first confirmed Lola had sent the head, and the second, that its malevolent tendencies were the product of rumour and over heated imaginations.

Life for Keith and Belinda slowly returned to normal. Well, as normal as it was ever going to be. It would not be right to say Duane was coming between them. Yet they both felt his presence. Belinda tried to treat him as an ornament or souvenir to be given an occasional dusting. But Keith felt he was still a friend. So he wished him a cheerful 'good morning' when coming down for breakfast. And an equally enthusiastic 'good night' on his way to bed. This began to irritate his wife. Especially when he forgot to give her the same greeting. They were happily married, and she was glad to have him home permanently since he retired. Now she began to realise, ridiculous as it seemed, she was becoming jealous of Duane. She was glad for small mercies. At least he was on top of the bookcase. Otherwise Keith would be patting him on the head every time he passed. And no doubt giving him a conspiratorial wink. She fought to control her feelings. It would be stupid to have rows about it. But when Keith suggested taking the skull with them on holiday, she exploded. Her anger shocked the engineer who'd only wanted to give it a change of scenery. He promised to come to his senses. Duane was hidden under a dish cloth and left behind. Yet two weeks after they returned, Keith took it off and again began his daily greetings.

At first they were whispered so as not to upset

Belinda. But it was not long before they reached their former level. She did not want another confrontation. Yet this new camaraderie between the pair began to eat away at her. She felt she had to talk to somebody. In the end she decided to confide in Reverend Pottie. She did not give the reason over the phone, but he guessed. And knew he would have to be on his mettle. He'd done his share of matrimonial counselling, but never where a third party was a decapitated head.

The tea tray lay on the table in the vicarage drawing room. There was nothing like a strong cuppa before an emotional discussion. Belinda sat on the edge of the sofa. Her heart seemed to have an irregular beat. She began to feel foolish. Could she think of an excuse to get up and leave? She felt her host's eyes on her. He had let her settle in silence but now spoke. "It is not easy to get things off your chest." Thinking as he said it, that hers wasn't bad for her age. He admonished himself quickly. He'd been having too many of those kind of thoughts lately. He put it down to the Spring weather.

"It's not an easy subject," came the reply. "It's that skull."

The vicar gave a sympathetic nod. "I thought it was."

She looked at him. "Did you? Yes, I suppose you did. It seems to be making its presence felt everywhere" Once started, she couldn't stop. It was as if the macabre interloper was still alive. Yet she knew he couldn't be. And that was what frightened her. She and Keith were a sane, normal, middle class couple not given to wild imagination. They did not believe in witchcraft. So why were they acting like this?

He stared at her gravely. "You do well to be frightened."

She gave a startled look. "What?"

"Just because we personally don't believe in something doesn't mean it doesn't exist. When I joined the Church of England, I was determined not to be narrow minded about faith. I studied other religions and cults and tried to look at our western ones from their point of view. Our ceremonies and beliefs can seem ridiculous to another's eye."

"Yes, but surely Duane wanting to be buried with Keith to be ready for the next world is over the top."

The Reverend Pottie raised his eyebrows. "What about our family plots in cemeteries? We do not speak about it, but subconsciously hope to journey on together. The thing everybody has in common, is the need to believe in something. Don't forget our god is invisible. At least those who worship the moon or the sun, can see theirs."

"Yes, but what about those spirits and spells? Do you really believe in those?"

The vicar poured them each a second cup. "I will tell you a story," he said. "And you can make up your own mind. Two boys in a poverty stricken West African village were playing football with a skull. They had no proper equipment. An elder warned them to stop or something awful would happen. Being young, they laughed and carried on. They were talented and later joined famous clubs. They had long forgotten the warning. Then one missed a vital penalty in a big match. He said his foot suddenly developed a mind of its own and hoofed the ball over the bar. The team lost thousands in prize money."

"He was obviously suffering from nerves," said Belinda.

"That's what I thought. Then I heard about the other one." The speaker helped himself to a biscuit but put it on his plate. He mustn't talk with his mouth full. Especially with his visitor's eyes trained on him. "He was famed for clearing the ball out of danger. Yet in a cup final, with no one near him, he headed it into his own net. He said his neck refused to obey his brain and inexplicably twisted the wrong way. His team too suffered the consequences of defeat."

Belinda frowned. "I know nothing about football, but that's complete nonsense. You can't possibly believe it was anything to do with that skull."

"I'm afraid I do. And so do both victims. They are adamant about this. They each realised instinctively its revenge had come."

"I don't read the sports pages, but I would have heard about such excuses as these."

"They're not the kind you publicise. They knew they would be ridiculed. So they only told close friends. One of whom was a pastor who related the saga to me at a church conference."

"It certainly is intriguing, but it doesn't prove anything."

"It does to me."

"Like what?"

"That you cannot dismiss such incidences out of hand."

"So you think Duane is responsible for my mother's coma and Mrs Strict's broken ankle?"

"I didn't say that. Yet I have to admit the fate of the footballers did come into my mind."

Belinda gave a deep sigh. "I came here for solace and support, but now I'm more worried than ever."

Her host clicked his tongue. "I'm sorry if I have let you down. I felt it more honest to tell you how I feel. Of course Duane could be harmless, only one must keep an open mind."

"So there is nothing wrong in Keith treating him as one of the family?"

"It's innocent enough apart from the effect it is having on you. Now you have made him aware of this, hopefully he will be more understanding."

His visitor rose to go. The whole thing had been a waste of time. The Reverend was obviously as mad as everybody else. She saw no point in stressing her fear of having the skull in their grave. That hopefully was many years off and a lot could happen in between.

Chapter 8

As the weeks passed, Duane faded into the background. Belinda had to give credit to Keith who became more distant towards his friend. At least when she was around. Even the villagers lost interest and talked about other things. So it was a shock when another letter from Lola arrived. Opening it gingerly, the engineer was confronted with a plea for help. The police were accusing her of robbing a grave. Could he confirm she was only carrying out her late husband's wishes? His wife, peering over his shoulder, looked confused. "But she's already done that for our force."

"Well, now we've got to do it for theirs."

"This is ridiculous."

Keith read on. "Her lawyer wants a photo as proof."

"Photo of what?"

"Me and the skull. And if possible, a policeman."

"A policeman?"

"Yes, to prove our boys have been on the case and checked the facts."

"But the Nigerian police know they have. Our force asked them to check first."

"This is for her defence. It looks like she's going to court."

Belinda closed her eyes in pure frustration. "Just forget the whole thing."

"We can't. Lola did what she thought was best, so we must not desert her."

"What are you going to do?"

"What she asks. We'll get inspector Howard. At least he knows the story. We'll need a plain background and Duane should be given a good polish."

His wife put her head in her hands. "I don't believe what I'm hearing."

42

"I'll send a letter of confirmation with the photo. That should do the trick. I don't see how anybody can be charged with desecrating their own family grave. Especially if they are carrying out the wishes of the deceased."

Picking up the phone, he got through to the station. He tapped his fingers restlessly. What was the best way to put his odd request? At least the inspector knew the background. The best thing was to tell it straight and simple. But the voice at the other end spoke first, and it sounded apologetic. "You're ringing about the photo are you?"

Keith could not hide his surprise. "Yes, as a matter of fact I am."

"My Nigerian colleagues have been on to me," explained the inspector. "They know Lola's lawyer wants one and asked if they could have a copy too. Just for their records. And while you're at it. We'll have one for ours."

The engineer felt his brain throbbing.

"It's only a couple of extra prints," added the voice. "Nothing could be easier."

Yes why not, thought his listener. And at the same time we can run off enough for all the village to have one.

"Are you still there?"

"Yes, I'm still here."

"Look, I'm sorry about this. You were right. The interview with Lola was anything but discreet. Six of them arrived in a police van. They were polite, but one thing led to another and now we have this desecration business. But it seems her account will be accepted, so we can relax."

Keith stiffened. Relax! Duane was leading them a merry dance.

43

"What about Wednesday?" asked the voice in his ear.

He looked blank. "Wednesday?"

"For the photo call."

"Oh that, yes."

"Ten thirty?"

"That will be fine."

The engineer replaced the receiver and looked at Belinda. "The Nigerian police and inspector Howard want pictures as well."

She paced up and down. "The whole thing is becoming more absurd by the minute."

"Everybody wants a record of the evidence these days."

"I can't believe all this hoo ha over a silly skull."

"It's not a silly skull. It's Duane's skull, and I hope he didn't hear you. He's only in the hall."

Belinda felt her anger rising. "I hope he did hear. And I meant every word of it. I'm fed up with worrying about hurting his feelings." She pointed a finger at herself. "What about mine? Don't they count for anything? Our lives have been turned upside down by that stupid parcel. I wish it had never arrived."

"Well it has, and we're stuck with it."

"We don't have to be stuck with it."

"Well, look what happened to your mother when she threw the skull away."

"You should have buried it in the garden as you first suggested. At least it couldn't stare at you there."

"It's perfectly all right on top of the bookcase."

"No, it shouldn't be in the house."

"Please calm down."

Keith went to put a comforting arm around his wife but she moved away. "I'm not saying either Duane goes or I go, but I'm warning you that time is not far off." Turning, she marched out of the room, slamming the door behind her.

Chapter 9

The inspector wore a smart grey suit with a crisp white shirt and red tie. Just the right amount of cuff was showing and his hair was perfectly parted. Yet Keith, handing Belinda the camera, sensed something was wrong. The pair were lining up with the skull between them when he realised what it was. "You're not in uniform."

His companion nodded. "I know I'm not. CID officers don't wear one."

"But anybody looking at the photo won't know you're a cop."

"The Nigerian police will."

"But what about when it's shown in court? It will lack conviction if you don't look the part."

The inspector gave a flicker of annoyance. "I suppose I should have thought of that. Anyway it's too late now." He suddenly brightened. "Wait a minute, I can hold up my warrant card." He began fishing in his pocket. "It's got quite a nice design."

Belinda tapped her foot impatiently as the pair admired, and then agonised, over the best angle to show this important exhibit. Finally they were ready. Should they smile? After all, Duane was grinning. They decided against it. It was a serious matter. Andre had suggested putting a cigar in the skull's mouth when the engineer mentioned the photo shoot in the pub. Keith had been cross, but could see it would have provided a certain charm.

Belinda's hand was steady and the resulting prints were deemed perfectly adequate. Their visitor left with three. Two for official sources and one to have pride of place on his mantelpiece. Just in case any of his friends refused to believe such a bizarre story.

"Well, that at last is that," said Keith returning the skull carefully to its perch.

"Do you really think so?" replied his wife who failed to hide her scepticism.

"I don't see why not. We've provided the proof required and the inspector authenticates it."

Chapter 10

"Did they like the photo?"

It was the first question Keith asked on picking up the phone to hear the inspector's voice. A month had passed without a single word about the affair.

"Yes they did. They liked it very much."

"Good."

"Yes, but not good enough."

"What do you mean?"

"They want the skull to appear in court as an exhibit and you as a witness."

The engineer was silent.

"Don't panic, you don't have to go. They won't try to extradite you. It's only a request."

His listener heaved an involuntary sign of relief. "That's all right then."

"But I think you should. You owe it to Lola, and there's trouble in her village. Its inhabitants claim a headless figure is terrorising them in the middle of the night."

"It's all in their imagination."

"Maybe, but they're convinced it's Duane. They believe he can't rest because his skull was removed without proper respect. Lola just hacked it off with a meat cleaver. They want it put back and then removed with proper ceremony. They have no objection to you taking it again as it's owner's last wish. You could have the whole skeleton, but you might need an export licence for it."

Keith struggled for breath. "This is very sudden. I'll have to talk to my wife."

"Yes, it must be a shock. Let me know what you decide."

Belinda appeared in the doorway. "Who was that?"

Keith went to the sideboard and poured two large gins. His wife watched in amazement. "What are you doing? We haven't had breakfast yet." Then it dawned on her. "It was that call, wasn't it?"

The engineer added a few splashes of tonic. "Yes, it was inspector Howard."

"What did he want?"

"He says I should go to Nigeria." He passed her a glass and related the conversation. She listened intently while taking several gulps. "You're right. It's not too early. We should be drinking round the clock." She poked her piece of lemon nervously. "It's impossible for you to go. It's far too dangerous."

"Why?"

"They'll charge you with receiving stolen goods."

"Of course they won't. It was a present."

"They won't see it that way if Lola's being done for desecrating a grave. And the villagers will blame you for Duane's ghost keeping them awake." She took another sip. "There's only one answer. We'll have to send the skull back on its own."

"We can't do that."

"Why not?"

"I say it again. Look what happened to your mother when she tried to part with it. I don't want to share her fate. And it might not just be me. It could affect you and everybody in the village."

"What? Every one of us in a coma? You're talking complete nonsense."

"I'm not prepared to risk it. A lot of odd things happen around that skull. Anyway, I owe it to Lola. She needs all the support she can get."

"You're far more likely to be a liability. You could both find yourselves in jail. And then what would you do?"

"You're being dramatic. I will be perfectly safe. I know the country well. I lived there for five years."

"But when you were last there, Duane was flesh and blood. Now he's a scary skull."

"Well he hasn't done any harm to me."

"Not yet he hasn't. I've just got a horrible feeling your turn will come."

Chapter 11

Keith agreed with Belinda a photo should be sufficient. Yet when Lola wrote again, he knew he had to go. Things were getting out of hand. The villagers were becoming paranoid. Duane's ghost was being seen in several places at once. And he was now waving his arms in threatening gestures. There had to be an exorcising ceremony, so could he bring the head? It was too risky posting it.

Keith had to agree. That night in the pub he revealed his impending departure. Belinda had insisted on going with him. So he was looking for someone to water their beans and tomatoes. And they could then eat them if they were not back in time. Although confident in front of her, he felt the trip would be far from plain sailing. Reggie promised to keep the engineer's own tankard hanging above the bar for at least six months. That did not make him feel any better.

Yet the landlord's mind was working hard. As the first to see the skull, he was proud of the kudos it gave him. He felt attached to it. So he decided he would escort Keith and Belinda. It had been years since he'd been abroad, and it would give him a chance to wear his favourite Panama hat. He kept his plan to himself. Maybe he was not alone? Over the next few days he would find out. There was nothing like safety in numbers.

Reggie discovered everyone was still fascinated by Duane. One by one, the rubbish tip searchers declared they would go too. It was as if something mysterious was pulling them along. Trish for example, found herself saying 'yes' when she meant to say 'no.' She was worried what might happen to her seagulll while she was gone. Joyce had hummed and hawed. But once

Sid promised faithfully he'd keep up, she'd thrown her hat into the ring. She'd feared he would lag even further behind in the tropical heat. Andre was all for it, but Reggie ordered him to go anyway. He did not want to leave him alone in charge of the pub. Rita and Tom were the most enthusiastic and started training immediately. They put the lounge central heating on full blast to simulate tropical conditions and then did several hundred circuits in singlets and shorts. They were not going to let the party down by wilting.

The Reverend Pottie was in a dilemma. Despite his claims to be open minded, the Church of England stalwart did not want to be seen escorting a skull to what was once the Dark Continent. So he suggested twinning their village with the Nigerian village. This would provide excellent cover for what was in reality, a macabre mission. The others agreed this was a masterstroke. And decided it was time to tell Keith so he could put forward the proposal. But first they would have their inoculations to make it a proper fait accompli. They had no idea how he would react.

The engineer was dumbfounded when the landlord appeared on his doorstep to break the news. He didn't know whether to be grateful or annoyed. Their show of support was impressive, but he felt they were muscling in on what was a private crusade. He realised he only had himself to blame. He had involved the whole community almost from the start. He had not been able to keep his mouth shut. In the end he knew he would be glad of their company. But if anything awful happened to them it would be on his conscience. He would do his best to make sure nothing did.

Luckily he had plenty of experience of the country. He could make sure they felt at home in their new surroundings and be welcome visitors. The most important thing was to learn the Niger Stomp. That was the villagers' favourite dance. He had often joined in himself to the great delight of his hosts. Once, with a bellyful of whisky, he'd done a solo to rapturous applause.

There were wry faces when he explained his plan, but he booked the village hall and they all turned up. He gathered them in a circle around him and gave a demonstration. It was just a case of bending one knee while stamping as hard as you can with the other foot. It looked tricky, but was easy to do with practice, although if you were not careful, it could give you backache.

The engineer simulated the necessary drum beat by taking off his shoe and banging it repeatedly against the wooden wall. Figures wobbled precariously as they flung themselves into the task. Andre, after much concentration, was the first one to get it right. He said it helped to pretend you were extinguishing an irritating cigarette end. Sid, stamping in unison with his wife, advocated putting on a dance of their own as a cultural exchange. His companions agreed enthusiastically and opted for the Hokey Cokey. Trying it out, Andre was again the star performer, and continued to practice in front of the mirror at home.

Keith next introduced the party to an array of native greetings. The best response, he said, was an enthusiastic smile and a vigorous nod. For their hosts who spoke English, a reply could be attempted. But not 'have a nice day' which was unknown in that part of the world. And certainly not 'All right squire?' as suggested by the young chef.

When it came to dress, the idea was to create a holiday mood. The natives liked bright colours. Hawaiian shirts featuring a banjo or drum were ideal.

Andre was ordered not to wear his Manchester United shirt.

Since the arrival of the Sky dish bringing Premier League football, the village to a man, supported Tottenham Hotspur. This was because the club's cockerel emblem closely resembled the head man's rooster.

A reply saying the village would be delighted to be twinned, arrived three days before the travellers were to depart. It sent everyone into a fever pitch of excitement. Now arose the question of who would be mayor. A figurehead was needed to greet their hosts' head man. Keith was the obvious choice but wanted to keep a low profile because of the skull. In the end the role went to Reverend Pottie. He was the next best candidate being tallest and having the gravest expression. The vicar put on a show of reluctance but inside felt he was the ideal man for the job. He hoped to add to his knowledge of other faiths while at the same time looking to make the odd conversion. But it was never easy talking about a god you couldn't see.

The next thing to be discussed was presents. Everybody wanted to take gifts of their own, but knew there would have to be one from the whole community. Andre with his catering experience suggested an ice cream making machine. They were bound to eat lots of it in the hot climate. Rita opted for an ornamental lamp post for the main street, but Tom said it would be difficult to carry and attract too many moths. Reggie thought the best idea would be a top of the range barbecue. Keith explained the villagers had cooked like that ever since the world began. After Trish went for a communal bicycle with a large shopping basket, the engineer called a halt. They would find a project the village wanted and help fund it.

The day of departure arrived. Clutching passports and sun hats, the party set off in the mini bus. They travelled light with one suitcase each. Inside Keith's, Duane was wrapped in a shirt and stuck at the bottom. Hopefully customs officials would not poke around in it at the other end. The visit was intended to last six days but Reggie parked in the airport's long stay car park. "You can't be too careful," he said.

Chapter 12

Ibi the head man beamed at Lola. So Mr Porter and his friends were arriving tomorrow. And they were bringing the skull. Soon everything would be fine. It would be reconnected to his skeleton and then removed again with proper ceremony. The exorcised ghost would no longer keep everybody awake. The villagers were so tired they were walking around half asleep.

The widow nodded with relief. She was worried the apparition would be a major weapon for the prosecution in court. If that was laid to rest, there would not be much of a case left. She had only carried out her husband's last wish and the villagers had loyally made no official complaint. It had just been the interfering police.

There was to be a great feast. The women would leave for the market at first light to get the best of everything. On the menu would be egg plant, bango soup, peppered stew and grilled gizzard. And lots of refreshing mango and banana sundaes.

Ibi's wife Beta was excused this duty. She would be busy pressing his best clothes. He couldn't decide between his yellow and green shirts. So she would do both. He would make a last minute choice depending on the weather. The green one looked better in the rain. He had been preparing his speech since the moment the visit was announced. Beta, his reluctant audience, knew every word of it in her sleep. She said if she heard it again she'd scream. And she kept her word, frightening the occupants of the neighbouring hut. Her husband was not put off. It would be his biggest occasion since addressing the basket ball team on the dangers of Lagos before they left for a national competition. That was two years ago and some had still to come back.

Ibi was tall with the reputation of being a flashy dresser. He was the first man in the village to wear an earring. But as with his shirts, dithered. He wore it in alternate ears until finally deciding on the left one. Much to the relief of his wife who was called upon to polish it every now and then.

The elders decided not to send a welcoming party to the airport. They were unused to the city lights and some might follow the example of the basket ball players. They would wait patiently at the entrance of the village. The visitors were to stay in the nearest hotel a few miles away and travel in daily by coach. Trish had wanted to sleep in the village, but a picture of a giant centipede in a guide book, changed her mind.

Villagers excitedly took up their positions as zero hour neared. Necks craned as the coach came into view. Perspiring faces inside, peered out with equal expectation. It was a momentous occasion. As it turned out, in more ways than one.

Lola had prepared a special place for the skull in her hut. She felt faint at the prospect of seeing part of her husband again. She forced her way to the front of the crowd. She could not spot the familiar features of the engineer. Yet he had promised to bring Duane. She watched the official greetings. The expressions were sombre. And none more so than Reverend Pottie's. Introduced to her by a worried looking Ibi, he spelt it out. Customs had opened Mr Porter's bag and found the head. He had explained his mission but they had not believed a word. Instead, they had congratulated him on his imagination. He was being held in custody charged with trafficking in human remains. The rest of the party could not stay at the airport, so had continued their journey. They felt they should consult their hosts before contacting the British Embassy.

As the news spread among the villagers, there were loud exclamations of dismay. These were followed by a subdued silence as the enormity of what had happened sunk in. Instead of Duane being joyously reunited with his skeleton he was locked in a customs safe. And what of the engineer? He had been a popular figure before returning to England. He faced the prospect of spending years in a grim jail. They would have to organise relays to take him food. They shuddered at the thought of the prison menu.

Everybody tried to lift each others' spirits. Yet nobody had an appetite for the mound of delicacies. The visitors, feeling good manners were at stake, picked listlessly at the offerings. It was then a taxi drew up in a cloud of dust. Out stepped Keith, clutching his suitcase and the skull. He had left the airport in too much of a hurry to repack it. The first person to see him was Andre. "It's Keith," he cried in delight. "And he's got Skulky."

"Don't call him that," the engineer hissed angrily. "It's disrespectful." Fortunately it had gone over the heads of those within earshot. He was immediately engulfed by a clamouring crowd wanting to know of his miraculous escape.

The officers had congratulated him on his imagination, but it transpired theirs was greater. On being interrogated more fully, he had revealed the fate of his mother-in-law and Mrs Strict. And for good measure, that of the forensic science technician. This had produced thoughtful looks. He said of course it was all nonsense, but he would not like to get on the wrong side of Duane. The skull should not be cooped up but instead joining his other bones. This added grave nods to the thoughtful looks. A whispered conversation followed. The engineer was led rapidly down a corridor to a small office where the head resided on a table. His two escorts did not seem keen to touch it. They stood well back as he picked it up with alacrity. A third officer opened an outside door for him where in the street, a fourth had already hailed a cab.

Barely a month ago, the English party would have laughed at such antics. But not any more. Oh no. As they looked at the skull with its gleaming yellow teeth, they felt it was a wise move. If any cargo should be labelled Handle With Care, this was it.

Yet its arrival immediately raised spirits. Now the carnival could begin. The night would be one long celebration. And so it was. The visitors, helped by large quantities of coconut wine, put everything into the Niger Stomp. The villagers much appreciated it, although Rita and Tom had to be dragged off the clearing which acted as a dance floor, when they ran out of encores. Their hosts then showed how it should be done before their guests took over with the Hokey Cokey. This they agreed later was a mistake. It should have been left for another evening. Most had spent all their energy on their previous effort and the night was hot. There were several crash landings with others tripping over prone bodies. This brought rapturous applause. Fortunately the onlookers believed it to be an authentic English ritual. The party ended up spending the night where they were. Andre was sick down the side of the coach and the driver sensibly drove off before anybody else followed suit. Despite their unexpected surroundings, everyone slept soundly.

An eerie silence hung over the village the next morning. Reggie, whose head was being attacked with vicious hammer blows, felt as if he was in a morgue. Sid, who still lay spread eagled on the dance floor, had a bucket of water thrown over him by Joyce. Looking for a silver lining, he realised at least he wouldn't be going shopping.

Grinning down on them all was Duane. He had been wedged in the lowest branch of what had been his favourite tree, so he could watch the celebrations. The villagers had joined in fully with their guests so nobody had stayed awake long enough to see if the ghost came out. Although many believed he hadn't appeared, being more relaxed now his head was back.

Despite their hangovers, a sense of urgency made them discuss Duane's future.

The question was a tricky one. Whether to re-inter and dig him up again before, or after, the court case where he would be the star exhibit. The majority were for doing it straight away. Especially the villagers. They felt the sooner it was done, the sooner the ghost would keep quiet. Another leading advocate was Belinda. She had been worried sick during her husband's incarceration and couldn't wait to see the skull underground again. Secretly she hoped it would never re-emerge but if it did, it would keep itself to itself.

A vote was about to be taken when Lola's lawyer arrived. Frank was squat with broad shoulders and a confident air. He wore a suit and tie whatever the temperature which gave him an extra touch of authority. He could understand their reasons for wanting to get the job done quickly, but warned it could rebound on them. Pacing up and down, he took on the role of prosecutor.

"Your Honour this skull has now been dug up not once, but twice. That is a double desecration. It increases the danger of the ghost remaining active and makes a mockery of a person's right to lie undisturbed in their final resting place. And not only that. The deceased was a proud man, and to have been posted as a parcel was particularly degrading. Especially as it was sent second class."

The Reverend Pottie intervened. The second raising, with adequate ceremony, would be to right the wrong caused by the first. That was without the proper ritual. This would correct the matter in the eyes of which ever god was watching from above.

Frank tried to hide his exasperation. "By digging up Duane twice you admit the first was a crime. Our defence is that it was a family affair with Lola faithfully honouring her husband's last wish. No other grave was disturbed and it was carried out at night so as not to upset anybody else's feelings. Admittedly using a meat cleaver lacked a certain finesse, but there was no other practical tool at hand."

Keith spoke for the first time. "So what do you suggest?"

"That we keep the head near to the body - say on top of the grave, until the hearing. That way we can demonstrate our respect by reuniting them as closely as possible without disturbing the rest of the skeleton. Then afterwards the proper ceremony can take place."

The engineer then revealed what was increasingly troubling him. "Is it essential that I appear in court?"

"It would be much better if you did."

"My wife thinks I could be done for receiving stolen goods."

"There is a risk of that, but I believe the danger is minimal. After all you co-operated with the police in both countries and voluntarily brought the head back. The only problem might be whether the court deems you showed enough respect for Duane. I see you took him to that bedridden widow in a John Lewis bag. I agree your reasons were honourable, but I suspect the judge, who was educated in London, would prefer him to have travelled in the Harrods one."

The engineer grimaced. "Will we have to go into all this?"

"I'm afraid we do. It is already in the public domain. You provided it in your interview with the English police who passed it on to ours."

"That means they know about the rubbish tip?" cut in Belinda.

"I'm afraid they do. But I shall plead most earnestly that your mother should not be extradited."

His listener's mouth fell open. "Extradited?"

"It is a distinct possibility."

"Just for throwing away a skull?"

"It may be a skull, but it is a Nigerian citizen. Or at least part of one."

"But he's dead."

"When you die you still belong to your country."

Keith had a vision momentarily of he and his mother-in-law in adjoining cells. The situation was becoming ridiculously out of hand. But to be fair, it had been from the moment Belinda had opened the parcel. If only it had got lost in the post. He forced himself to concentrate. On balance Duane had been treated with respect. They'd thrown a party for him to meet the neighbours and both he and the inspector had worn suits for the court photograph. Admittedly he had travelled stuffed in a suitcase in the hold of the plane. Yet he could hardly have gone as hand luggage. It could have upset the other passengers.

He looked at Frank who took a silk handkerchief from his breast pocket and mopped a dampened brow. He would have to rely on him. There was no other option. He certainly seemed to know his onions. Or, as they no doubt said in Nigeria, mangoes. There seemed to be a good chance of an acquittal. And if there wasn't? He preferred not to think about that outcome.

It was finally decided to follow the lawyer's advice. So how to store Duane on top of his grave? Somebody suggested using an abandoned fridge lying on the edge of the clearing. This was hastily vetoed as was a meat safe and the box which brought the Sky dish to the village.

What was needed was something more upmarket. Something with a bit of class. There was a further scratching of heads. Ibi then said they would build a house for Duane. It would be his shrine - something that would go down well in court. When volunteers were called for, a forest of hands shot up. Or rather crept up. Most of their owners were still suffering from the previous night's effects. There were white hands as well as black. The English party were determined to be involved. They had not come all this way just to be spectators in such a drama. Tom and Sid had done a little carpentry and Trish considered herself a nifty hand at murals.

Everybody escorted the working party into the jungle to find the right pieces of wood. The exercise helped them sweat out the last of the coconut wine. Soon sporadic singing broke out from the natives coupled with bursts of chanting. The visitors responded with Ten Green Bottles which was the nearest equivalent they could think of. They continued to swap tunes until Andre's solo version of Get Off My Cloud caused interest to wane. He annoyed Keith by dedicating it to Skulky but mercifully once again this passed unnoticed.

By early evening the task was finished. The four foot square box with its straw roof and open front, was reverently manoeuvred into place. Patu the witch doctor danced round it several times muttering incantations in a high pitched voice. As it was a joint venture, the vicar asked if he could contribute. He would understand if the offer was refused. But no, the village was greatly honoured. Two faiths were better than one. And they hoped his dance would be as entertaining as the witch doctor's. Faces fell when he explained his Church didn't caper about, but sang a lot. Realising he had unwittingly put himself in a corner, he cancelled the blessing and launched into the Lord Is My Shepherd. Despite his urgings, the rest of the party steadfastly refused to join in. As Andre whispered, Skulky would have liked something more lively.

With everything ready, Lola collected her husband's head from her hut. Kissing the top of it devotedly, she carefully put it inside on a small piece of cloth. The box stood three feet above the rest of the skeleton. The young chef said Skulky must feel like a giraffe. He did not catch the engineer's reply, which was just as well. It had something to do with being put on the next plane home.

Reggie suggested posting sentries, but Keith said no, it was not Buckingham Palace and who would steal Duane? And they were unlikely to find volunteers among their party. Nobody would want to stand around in the hot sun ceaselessly swotting flies. Even so the shrine was kept under surveillance. Everybody walking past found their eyes drawn unwaveringly towards it. Trish had painted a palm tree on each side under a deep blue sky. It was a good effort considering she used local materials which she then couldn't get off her hands.

Although Duane was only semi connected, his two parts were close enough to give him a feeling of togetherness. At least that's what the villagers thought.

The headless ghost had vanished. There was much sage nodding and glances of approval directed at the shrine. Duane was back in his home. Well, the annexe anyway.

Chapter 13

In the days running up to the court hearing, the English party retired to their hotel at night and returned in the morning. They missed the village atmosphere but not enough to forego hot showers and clean sheets. The thought of sleeping at eye level with a host of insects was unnerving. But they gradually became used to these. As long as they didn't crawl straight at you. The one thing they couldn't yet stomach, was seeing them on a plate. Either fried or grilled. They lived in fear they would be on the menu of the next feast. And knowing they would have to take at least one bite for the sake of good manners.

The culture change was not all one way. Andre in a rash moment, offered to cook shepherd's pie for the entire village. It took several women two hours to cut the mutton small enough to resemble mince. And there was only sweet potato for the topping. The appreciative smiles when it was served quickly turned into thoughtful expressions. The chef himself admitted it was chewy and apologised for the flies that had somehow got in.

Keith happily watched the mingling of the two communities. It had been a good idea of Reggie's for everybody to come. True, it had worried him at first. Yet nobody had caught a horrible disease or trodden on a poisonous snake. The worst that had happened, was Rita being trapped inside a hut for two hours by a sunbathing lizard. She said it had kept looking at her.

Yet the engineer's pleasure was mingled with apprehension. The court case was a dark cloud hanging over his head. The whole thing was surreal. Despite all that had happened, he could not believe the skull was anything but a harmless piece of bone. The lengthy series of incidences could be rationally explained if examined individually. It was when you lumped them together that things looked different. As Belinda said, it was enough to make the hairs stand up on the back of your neck.

His mind went back to when there had been plenty on Duane's. When alive, he'd been such a likeable chap. It was impossible to believe him being so vindictive when dead. Keith shrugged his shoulders. But of course he hadn't been. It was all his imagination. And there would no room for that it in the calm atmosphere of the court house. That would be a good thing. But what would happen afterwards? Nobody had really thought about that. Even if things went smoothly the skull would remain a problem. He was committed to taking it back to England. But what if he needed an export licence? Or Duane might even be made a ward of court. Anything was possible.

The engineer knew if he was honest, he secretly hoped he would be barred from taking the skull. That would solve everything. Yet would Duane hold him responsible? Would he think he had tried hard enough? And that would involve the whole English party. They all knew of his previous victims and would be nervous he would wreak his revenge. They would refuse to get on a plane in case it crashed. Or a boat in case it sank. They would be trapped in Nigeria. And even if they risked a ferry across the smallest stretch of sea to Europe, they would shun trains for the same reason. And coaches. It would be an incredibly long walk home. And like a convoy, they could only move at the speed of their slowest member. He imagined Joyce finally having to put Sid on a lead. The whole scenario was horrific.

And his mood was not improved when Frank drew

him quietly aside. Had he got any medical problems? Heart murmurs, diabetes, hardening of the arteries? The engineer looked puzzled. "What do you mean?"

"Any mitigating circumstances?"

"Mitigating circumstances?"

"In case."

"In case of what?"

"In case you're found guilty of harbouring a stolen skull."

"You said we were certain to be acquitted."

"It's only insurance. We have to be ready for every kind of verdict."

"By this one you mean prison?"

"I'm sure it wouldn't be for long, but as I said, it's highly unlikely."

"It doesn't sound like that."

Frank ignored the implication and went on. "It would help if we could say you are not too well. They don't like people to die in the cells. It gives the jail a bad name."

"I can't think of anything. I'm pretty fit for my age. Although I'm not feeling as good as I was a moment ago."

"Maybe we could get Patu to help. He's the best witch doctor for miles around. He has a whole series of spells. He could put you under one for a few hours. You know, make your jaw go slack so you couldn't answer awkward questions. Or he could cross your eyes and make you dribble."

"That's very kind, but I prefer to take my chances. I'm sure the judge will reach the correct and sensible decision."

Frank fingered his tie which was blue with bright red spots. "Talking of judges, there is one more thing."

Keith gave a heavy sigh. In Africa, there was always

one more thing.

"We have to avoid appearing before His Honour Babi Basutu at all costs."

"Why, what is it about him?"

"He has great reverence for the dead. He automatically gives grave robbers the most severe sentences. It started when his great grandmother was dug up. She was reputed to have wonderful healing powers. So the thieves ground down her bones to put in their soup."

"But it is different with Lola. She was carrying out her husband's last wish."

Frank raised his eyebrows. "Can you prove it?"

"Of course I can."

"How?"

"She alone knew what he wanted. Nobody else in the village knew. In fact only the three of us did."

"She could have secretly sold you the skull. You knew her well from your time in Nigeria and could have become fascinated by its dark arts. Many people are enthralled by such heads and keep them for all sorts of bizarre uses."

"But what about the letter that came with it? It clearly shows her intentions."

The lawyer gave a snort of contempt. "Pure cover for the real reason."

Keith shook his head. "This is becoming all beyond me. Nothing seems to make sense anymore."

Frank put an arm round the engineer's shoulders. "Enjoy the moment man. Life is always exciting in Africa."

Chapter 14

The English party for their gift, decided to fund a new school house. But they could not afford to cover the entire cost. It was Ibi who came up with the idea of how to get the extra money. Word of Duane had reached surrounding villages and his fame was growing steadily. Everybody wanted to come and have a look. The head man had at first been protective, but then thought why not? It could be an excellent way of raising revenue. A small charge would be made to view the head. And from the numbers expected, this would easily cover the extra amount.

Keith's first instinct, like Ibi's, was that the venture was repulsive and disrespectful. Yet he too gradually warmed to it. Especially when Ibi unfolded the second part of his plan. Viewing would start as soon as the court case was over, and would become a permanent event. The engineer would lend the skull on a long term lease until he died. Duane would then be despatched with all speed so they could both be interred together. The problem was to ensure he did not feel left behind when the Englishman returned home. So wrapping paper and a label prominently bearing Keith's address, would be put next to him in the shrine. That way he'd know what his final destination would be.

The villagers and their guests unanimously agreed this was the best solution. Andre suggested making the shrine the centre of a theme park. Skulkyland could have children's rides with blow up crocodiles and giant earwigs. He was enthusiastically supported by Trish who volunteered to paint animals on all the huts. Keith, who had winced at the title, vetoed the idea. It was not Disneyland. It had to be done in the African tradition. Visiting a shrine should be a dignified affair. He was backed up by Ibi who was grateful for such a show of sensitivity.

Yet even the head man's mind was becoming alert to one or two opportunities. Every site had its mementoes. There was nothing wrong with a few nick knacks. Especially replica skulls if they were tastefully done. These could be large, medium or small - to fit every pocket. They would be a fine adornment to any abode. And they would be accompanied by a dusting cloth and a brush for the teeth. To keep such a valuable acquisition in top condition. They could be sold in a union jack bag to signify Duane's visit to England. Yes, such things would enhance the product. There must of course be nothing tacky to harm the reputation of the village. That was one thing he would make sure of.

Keith meanwhile wondered what Belinda would make of the new arrangement if he died first. She had made it clear she did not like the idea of the head joining them. So would she carry out the plan or double cross him? He decided it was too far into the future to worry about.

Chapter 15

It was the night before the court case that Duane disappeared. He was there at ten o'clock when Ibi looked in to say goodnight. Yet in the morning he was gone. Lola, intending to wish him a cheerful 'good morning,' found the empty shrine lying discarded a few yards from the grave. Her shriek brought horrified figures tumbling from their huts, soon to be joined by the arriving English party. There were many open mouths and much scratching of heads, Andre summed up what all were thinking. "Who would want to nick a crazy skull?" he exclaimed. Nobody had the faintest idea. One or two of the more superstitious, wondered if the headless ghost had collected his property.

Without its prize exhibit, the hearing was adjourned. Despite Frank's indignant denials, the prosecutor declared it was a delaying tactic. He informed the police and a busload arrived to commandeer a hut for their search headquarters. Everybody in the village and those beyond were under suspicion. Anybody could have taken it. With nobody keeping watch, the thief or thieves, had seven hours of darkness to operate in.

Inspector Howard with his intimate knowledge of the English suspects, was flown out to help. He greeted Keith with a shake of his head. "You're in a right pickle."

"I know. But I promise you none of our group took the skull. And I feel the same way about the villagers. Duane's reputation has spread for miles, so it has to be somebody from outside."

"You can't be sure without proof. That's the first thing a detective learns. It's the same in any country."

"But why would anybody here want to do it? We're all desperate to get the court case over with. It's been

72

hanging over our heads for far too long. Then the village can open the shrine and start earning an income."

The new arrival fanned himself with his warrant card. "Do you mind if I take my jacket and tie off?"

"Go ahead, and your socks too if you like. This climate takes a bit of getting used to."

The inspector hung the discarded items over the branch of a tree. They were sitting in its shade on the edge of the clearing. "Well, who do you think did it?"

"I honestly haven't a clue. As I said, it could be a complete stranger. But you can tell your Lagos colleagues they can disregard our hosts. They are terrified the headless ghost will now return."

"Oh, it's still hanging around is it?"

"Yes, the locals believe he can't rest without his skull. It stopped when it was put on top of his grave. No doubt it was all down to their imagination, but it seems real enough to them."

His companion removed an ant from his armpit. "I agree that puts a different complexion on it. They certainly appear to lack a motive. And so do your lot. After all, you came here to return it safely. It's got all the makings of a mystery that will never be solved. They've found a host of finger prints on the box but lots of people have peered in. Likewise the ground is well trampled." The speaker mopped his brow. "You haven't got a spare pair of shorts have you? I'll never get used to this heat."

"I'm afraid I haven't."

"I came out in such a rush I didn't have time to get anything tropical. But I don't see what the hurry was. There's an immediate dead end."

"But what do your counterparts think? They should understand the minds of their countrymen."

"Roughly the same as me. Their main suspect is Patu. They believe the witch doctor made the skull disappear. I would have laughed at that before all this business started. Now I am not so sure. The problem is they're too scared to give him a hard time in case he puts a spell on them. Yet as you said, what's the motive?"

"Exactly, there isn't one."

The engineer felt a sudden wave of panic at being trapped. The court case would eventually go ahead even if the skull wasn't found. It could take months, and it was unlikely he would be allowed to leave the country before then. He was in limbo and so was the whole village.

The days dragged by and even the police appeared to be only going through the motions. The English party began to think of going home. Reggie in particular was worried how the White Hart was faring under a temporary manager. Yet as Keith had predicted, they were edgy about any departure upsetting Duane. Wherever he was. Unlike the others, the engineer had taken to staying in the village and had been given a room at the back of Lola's hut. It was there he awoke one morning to find a crumpled note beside his bed. Whoever had placed it, had crept in very stealthily for he was a light sleeper. It said: MEET ME TONIGHT BY THE BANYAN TREE. COME ALONE. He knew the spot. It was a few hundred yards outside the village reached by a little used path. But who had written it? And why? He puzzled over it all day. He suspected it was either Ibi or Patu. They both seemed to be giving him sly glances. But why couldn't they speak to him quietly if they needed to? Or maybe it wasn't them? It was just his imagination. He decided not to mention his find to anyone. Not even Belinda who had noticed his preoccupation and was giving him quizzical looks.

As the short twilight turned into night, his heart began to beat faster. The note had not said a time, but he decided on eleven o'clock. His party would be safely back at their hotel by then and the villagers turning in. Shortly before the appointed hour he slipped out of his room and skirting round the edge of the huts, found the track. The moon was up and it was easy to follow. In ten minutes he reached his destination. Yes, it was the right tree, but nobody was there. He settled down to wait. An hour passed. The jungle rustled around him but he was unperturbed. He was well used to its sounds. He constantly wracked his brain as to who his visitor might be. That was if he was to have one. The minutes ticked away with no hint of an approaching figure. Then suddenly a voice came to him out of the darkness. It had a familiar tone.

"I'm sorry Keith about causing a little trouble."

The engineer staggered and caught a nearby branch for support. "Duane?"

"Yes, it's me."

"It can't be, Lola sent me your skull."

"No, mine is still firmly on my neck." He stepped into a patch of moonlight. "Look."

His dumbfounded companion stared at the apparition. He did indeed look every inch his friend. Unless it was a double. The prominent teeth, the mischievous grin, the grizzled hair. They were all there along with his familiar gait as he ambled towards him and stuck out a hand. The engineer took it, wondering if he was confronting a ghost. But he was definitely grasping flesh and blood. The fingers were as firm as ever. He found himself leaning against the tree. His legs felt weak and he was breathing heavily. His brain struggled to take in what was happening. Then a reassuring arm came round his shoulder. "A bit of a shock, eh?"

Somehow Keith got the words out. "Shock? You nearly killed me." His heart was thumping loudly inside his shirt.

"I was going to stay quiet, but I could see things were getting out of hand."

His listener's eyes widened in astonishment. "Out of hand? Do you know what you have done? You've disrupted the lives of two communities and landed your wife and me in court. We could both go to jail and my mother-in-law too for good measure."

"It was never meant to happen like this."

"Is that all you can say? It was never meant to happen like this?"

"Well, it wasn't. How was I to know Lola would carry out that ridiculous last wish."

"What? You didn't mean her to?"

"I did at the time. When I got home I begged her to do it. But when I sobered up I forgot all about it."

"Me too."

Keith looked puzzled. "Then how did it happen? I mean sending your skull while at the same time keeping it on your shoulders?"

Duane settled himself against the base of the tree and told his story. He had a secret girlfriend in Lagos. He visited her several times a month, telling his wife he was doing overtime on the rigs. What he did not know, was that Paula had another lover. This man was a vicious criminal, the leader of a notorious gang in the city. He surprised Duane in her arms. A fight broke out and carried on into the street. His rival slipped and banged his head on the pavement. With blood pouring from a deep wound, it was obvious he had little time to live. Before the ambulance arrived, Duane was able to swap clothes with the man and leave his rig security passes in the breast pocket for identification. The victim of what was presumed to be a hit and run driver, died the following morning and the rig and Lola were duly informed. Duane had hidden behind a clump of bushes to watch his own funeral and then started a new life with his girlfriend. The unsuspecting gang members puzzled over their leader's disappearance but never reported it to the police. He was on the most wanted list and they did not relish drawing attention to themselves. Duane could hardly adopt his infamous identity, but did risk wearing the Rolex watch he had taken from his rival along with his dark glasses and crocodile skin shoes. Without papers, he survived by doing odd jobs and lived happily with Paula.

Keith's brow darkened. "But what about that dent at the back of your head where the coconut landed? That's how I identified you."

"That's exactly the place where his head hit the pavement. When I wiped away the blood I could see it. It was a perfect match. We were the same height and build so I jumped at the chance."

"But what about Lola? She was an excellent wife."

"She was, but man, this one is twenty years younger. You know, firm and supple. Nothing sagging."

"But the physical side isn't everything."

Even in the darkness, Keith could sense his friend's pitying gaze upon him. He shifted his position. "So why did you take the skull?"

"I didn't."

"Then who did?"

"Members of his gang,"

Keith struggled to come to terms with what he was

hearing. "How did they know where it was?"

"Paula. She felt guilty over his death although I killed him. She felt he should be with his gang. She's friendly with one of their girlfriends and tipped her off."

"Doesn't that put you in danger?"

"No. She just said where to find him. Not how he got there."

" But why would they want it now?"

"As I said, Vincent was a famous bandit. Vincent the Knife to give him his full name. If any robbery takes place and the culprits aren't found, he automatically takes the blame. And there have been a string of these lately. The police think he is lying low, so they have placed a huge reward on his head." The speaker paused before adding: "dead or alive."

"But he's already dead."

"Exactly, but the reward still stands."

"Then -."

"Yes, the skull is worth a hundred thousand kobos. That's a small fortune here"

"But how will they know it's him?"

"DNA, it's the big thing now."

"Well if the gang's got it, they can claim the money."

"It's not that easy. Whoever hands it in is bound to be fully investigated. Its members will risk having their association with Vincent discovered. Then they would find themselves arrested. At the moment they will be trying to come up with a solution. That will give us time."

The engineer had a sense of impending disaster. "Time for what?"

"Time to get the head back."

"Who's going to do that?"

"Your English party."

"Are you kidding? That lot against highly efficient, ruthless cut throats? What's wrong with the men of your village doing it? Or even a rival gang. We could pay commission."

"No, if we use fellow Nigerians it will lead to feuds and widespread gang warfare. With the English, once it is done you will go straight home."

"And how are we supposed to do this?"

"We will find a way."

"It's impossible. What you need are special forces. We're like the Home Guard. We're a bunch of senior citizens including four women. Add to that an irresponsible teenager, an overweight publican, and a vicar who's a pacifist, and you have a recipe for a massacre."

Duane's voice adopted its brightest tone. "They have got the brawn, but you have got the brains."

"I don't think we've got enough of them." He ran his mind over his assembled troops. "No, definitely not. There's not enough speed of thought, let alone speed of foot."

"All we need is a plan."

"That's easy to say, but I don't believe there is one with an earthly chance of success. And anyway, why would my party want to get it back? With all the trouble it's caused they will be glad to be rid of it. Especially when they learn it belongs to Vincent the Knife and is not yours. That explains its horrible behaviour. I couldn't believe it was you doing all those nasty things. You were far too nice."

His listener nodded in appreciation. "Thank you for being kind but we must keep it a secret."

"Keep what a secret?"

"That it's not my skull. Otherwise of course your

party will be reluctant to help. Even for some of the money. I know you English are quite well off."

Keith shook his head. "I can't do that. I can't lie to my friends."

"You don't have to. Just don't say anything. That's not lying."

"It is to me."

Duane reached out in the darkness and took his friend's arm. "This is really important. The reward could transform my village."

"Yes, but they will have to know the truth."

"Everybody can afterwards."

"But what about you? You will still be here and the gang will want revenge. And what will Lola say?"

"They do not know I killed Vincent. They know nothing about me. They will curse the English but you will be far away."

"But Lola?"

"She will not find me in Lagos."

The engineer felt a headache coming on. "Let me get this straight. I tell my party a highly organised criminal gang has stolen your skull. When they ask why would they want to do that? I say I haven't a clue. Then if by a miracle we succeed in getting it back, I say sorry, I was confused, it's not Duane's, it's Vincent's. We've got to hand it in to the authorities to gets lots of money."

Duane nodded. "And then of course, there's the rest of the skeleton."

"What?"

"That has to be handed in too. To get the full reward. It will be easy to dig it up."

The engineer put his head in his hands. "This is complete nonsense. I'm going mad. I need to see a psychiatrist."

"Keith, you know Africa well. It's only a little problem."

The engineer felt his anger rising. "A little problem? A nuisance?" His raised voice sent two startled bats winging over his head.

"Sssh," commanded his friend. "You'll wake the village."

"Wake them? I'll more than wake them. It's time we came clean with everybody. Put all our cards on the table."

Duane became agitated. "No, no Lola will kill me."

"Then we really can have your skull on our bookcase."

"What?"

"Nothing."

"Keith, we must keep this to ourselves. It's the only way."

But the engineer's mind was made up. "No, tomorrow morning I will summon everyone together and tell them the complete facts. They will of course think I am crazy. But then you will appear -."

"And they will think they are crazy. It will be too much of a shock."

"No it won't if I prepare them properly."

"I know my people. They will believe it's witchcraft."

"They can believe what they like, but they will see you are flesh and blood. Then we can all plan together on the best way to get the head back."

Duane could see his friend would not budge. "All right. If it must be, it must be. But on one condition."

"What's that?"

"You must keep Lola away. Send her shopping."

"I can't do that. I can't leave her out."

"I know what she's like when she's angry. She'll

attack me with her cooking ladle. I tell you it hurts."

You deserve it."

"But I must reappear with dignity, and I can't do that if she's hitting me over the head. She'll chase me and I'll be a laughing stock."

"Then stand your ground."

"That's inviting suicide. You don't know Lola."

"I'll have a word with Ibi. I'm sure we can quietly disarm her before your arrival."

"Well don't forget her other weapons. Especially the club she uses for grinding grain."

"We can't clear out the whole hut."

"She is a woman who can attack you with anything."

"It's only fair she should be there, so you'll have to take your chance."

The pair parted with Duane reluctantly promising to make what would be a highly dramatic appearance at noon. That should give Keith enough time to break the news of his friend's second coming. And just how to do that was vigorously exercising his brain as he made his way back along the track.

Chapter 16

The coach from the hotel arrived promptly at nine that morning. The engineer watched its passengers disembark. He felt the sweat trickle down his neck. It was far from the hottest part of the day, but it was not only the heat affecting him. It had seemed so simple when sitting under the tree in the darkness. He would calmly call his group together and tell them Duane was alive. Just like that. Now he couldn't find the words. He had intended to inform the villagers at the same time, but the size of the crowd would have been too intimidating.

Once the English knew, he would quietly brief Ibi who could pass it on to his people in the way he thought fit. And he no doubt, would have a much harder job. He took a deep breath. It was a case of the sooner the better. Or his nerve might fail him completely. He called the party over to a shady spot a little way from the huts. He intended to keep it simple without making it too much of a shock. They looked at him expectantly.

"Duane sends his regards."

There were a few wrinkled brows.

He tried again. "I saw Duane last night. He said to say 'hello.'"

Reggie was the first to speak. "Duane who?"

"Our Duane."

"Don't be silly," declared Andre, "Skulky's dead."

The engineer ignored what for the young chef, was an imminently sensible remark. Things were not going to plan. Nobody had asked what Duane was doing coming back from the grave. The fact obviously wasn't sinking in. He made another attempt. "Duane will be appearing here at noon today."

"Nonsense," replied the vicar. "Only Jesus rises again. We all know that."

The engineer's voice was firm. "Duane never rose from anywhere. He never died."

Trish was the first to begin to get the picture. "So whose skull has been terrorising us then?"

Keith shot her a grateful glance. "Vincent the Knife's."

Her face clouded. "Vincent who?"

Now he had their attention, he plunged on. The words came tumbling out. His audience listened spellbound. When he had finished, nobody uttered a sound. They stared in amazement at one another. Finally Tom fingering his sweat band, said: "It's a joke isn't it?"

But Belinda who knew her husband, swiftly intervened. "Oh no, if Keith said Duane will be there, he will be."

The others too began to be convinced. Extraordinary as it was. The broke into an excited chatter. The engineer felt a surge of relief. He had feared the worst but there was an upbeat mood. The African adventure was continuing. He had not mentioned the small detail of tackling the criminal gang. That could wait until later. First they must be introduced to Duane. And have a good laugh over the antics of what they had thought was his skull.

But now Ibi must be told. He found the headman eating a mango by the stream. He let him finish in case the news made him choke on it. Yet his listener was calmness himself. He took it all in his stride. It was a typical Duane trick. The men would nod and shrug their shoulders after giving a hearty chuckle. But he would not involve the women. No, they would side with Lola. He wouldn't warn her or them. That would spoil the entertainment. As for the cooking ladle, better to leave it where it was. Otherwise the maddened wife might reach for her meat cleaver.

Keith watched Ibi wander off to discreetly spread the word among the males. The engineer marvelled at the blatant sex discrimination. At home the head man would be straight before a tribunal. He looked at his watch. An hour and a half to go. Was he right to have forced Duane into a corner? After all, his friend had once saved his life. Yet he knew he was. A time comes when all must be revealed. It was the only way to have any hope of success. He wondered how the old rascal was feeling because that was how he now saw him. Lots of men left their wives for younger women but none had caused such havoc. It had even threatened his own marriage. And as far as he could see, the drama was far from over.

The minutes ticked away. A crowd began to gather. First the English party and then the local men. Inevitably word reached the ears of the women. They joined the throng jostling by the track that led into the village. That was the way Duane would come. Wedged in among them was Lola, who Keith was relieved to see was empty handed.

Midday arrived but there was no sign of the visitor. People were standing on tiptoe, peering down the track, their hands shading their eyes against the sun. Yet it remained doggedly empty. Murmurs of dismay began. The onlookers felt cheated. Glances were thrown at the engineer. Why had they believed such a fantastic story? He shifted his feet uncomfortably. Had his friend chickened out? No, surely not. That was not like him. Yet he had to face the facts. Duane wasn't there. Then he heard his name being called. And by that familiar voice. It came from over his head. He looked up into the tree above him at the edge of the clearing. A face appeared through the foliage. "It's me."

Keith craned his neck. "What on earth are you doing up there?"

"Lola - it's safer."

Soon every pair of eyes swivelled in his direction. Duane edged along a branch until his top half came into view. Holding on with one hand, he gave his audience a wave with the other.

"Duane! Duane!," they cried. "Is it you?"

"Yes, yes, it's me."

"Where have you been?"

"I have been in Lagos."

"Who with?" shouted the local men.

"With a friend."

"Is she pretty?"

The fugitive waved a finger as if to say 'enough.' but it was already too much for Lola. The lowest limb was out of reach but sympathetic female friends hoisted her up and she clasped it firmly. Duane was deciding whether to stamp on her fingers or climb higher when Ibi intervened. There must be no domestic violence unless it occurred within the huts. The village had its reputation to think of. Summoning Patu, they each grasped an ankle and pulled. Lola hung on like grim death but their extra strength told and she came crashing down. This set the women wailing and the men laughing while the English party looked on with mouths agape.

Keith closed his eyes. This was exactly what he didn't want. A farce. If things became too ridiculous his group would give up and go home before finishing the job. Yet the skull's fate was still the best deterrent. They were still nervous of it. Especially now knowing it belonged to a vicious killer. If they deserted it, it might well do something really nasty. Better to wait for it to be reunited with its skeleton and interred in a civilised fashion.

Duane meanwhile, found it hard to be heard from the top branch. He was coaxed to a lower level after Ibi and Patu promised to guard Lola. The errant husband told how he had accidentally killed the gang leader without feeling it necessary to say he had been found in Paula's arms. He revealed the reward and how it would benefit the village. An excited buzz ran through the crowd. And it increased in tempo when he explained the English party had promised to get back the skull. This of course was news to them. They fixed incredulous looks upon Keith who in turn glared at the speaker who was in full flow and failed to notice. The engineer found himself overwhelmed by villagers vying to shake his hand. The same thing was happening to the other members of his group. Some were even slapped on the back by the more exuberant of their hosts. The engineer forced himself to look on the bright side. It was a very neat fait accompli. His companions could not get out of helping now.

Yet if he had one wish, it was that the branch holding Duane would snap, sending him hurtling to the ground. Then they could take it in turns to stamp on him. No, he would leave it to Lola. He would go and fetch her cooking ladle for her. Or hopefully the meat cleaver.

But when he calmed down, he saw the fugitive had done his job for him. The party might complain he'd kept the plan secret, but they knew the score now. That of course was the easy part. Carrying it out was quite another matter.

It was Rita who came up with the solution. They would be a dance troupe. Their first night effort at the village had been a great success. They would repeat it and add the Lambeth Walk and the Charleston to their repertoire. She had once wanted to be a Bluebell girl in Paris and intended doing a duet with Tom. The idea was to put on a show at the sprawling tenement where the gang lived. This was on the outskirts of Lagos and within easy reach. Its members were bound to love any kind of dancing and were sure to attend. Paula knew the girlfriend of one of them and had told Duane the skull was being kept on the third floor. At the height of the performance, someone, yet to be decided, would sneak up and steal it.

Unsurprisingly there were no volunteers for this task. Andre knew he was the most likely candidate being the youngest and fittest. He had developed a limp as insurance, and was heard muttering he had no head for heights. He suggested serving his shepherd's pie in the interval laced with a laxative. This would give whoever went for Vincent's head, a clear run. It was sensibly vetoed. The atmosphere would suffer if the audience suddenly disappeared en masse at speed.

Trish promised to draw posters which Duane would see were put up in the district beforehand. Still marooned in the tree by Lola's enraged presence, he was joining in the discussion through his mobile. It would be five hours before overcome by tiredness, she nodded off allowing him to climb down and escape. She awoke to shout after him. "You wicked, wicked man, we will meet again." He shook his head strenuously as he ran, but knew somehow they would.

The troupe rehearsed in the cool of the evening. There were too many flies during the day. If you swatted them, you got out of step. Reggie's plea to include the Twist was turned down. Most of them were over sixty and were flinging themselves around enough as it was. Rita tried dancing in bare feet. She felt it would be appreciated, but the experiment ended after she squashed a cockroach. This was a relief for Tom who had been urged to take his own shoes off. Sid's Lambeth Walk was a crawl, but he refused to be left out despite Joyce's offer to dance for two. Rita felt the over confident pensioner couldn't dance for one, but kept quiet. They were in it together and team spirit was vital. The vicar struggled with his two left feet, but so did everybody when they drank coconut wine. Yet it helped them relax. They could never take to the floor sober. That was out of the question. But how much should they drink? Local brews were cheap but very morish. One could become two or three. Or if you were feeling really good, four. Most of the troupe could knock back plenty but Keith put a limit of two. It was no good falling down drunk. Apart from anything else, having to be dragged to the coach could hinder a quick get away.

Slowly their efforts bore fruit. Rita's arm flinging required extra space, but the dances were recognisable as coherent movements. A rehearsal staged for the village went without a hitch. Belinda who saw herself as the choreographer, was delighted. But the applause was muted this time. The onlookers were listless with some looking distinctly bored. A puzzled Keith asked Ibi why. The answer was simple. Not enough zoom and boom.

So while the dancers rested, the engineer topped up their glasses. The two only rule had been a mistake. What was needed were collisions and plenty of skidding about to enliven the routines. The interval was extended as he went round with a second bottle. Then it was time for the finale. Rita was pawing the ground like a young filly. Joyce imitated a swaying totem pole as Sid circled her like an Apache. Their antics lit up the crowd. This was more like it. One of two near the front, could not contain themselves and joined in. Then more followed. Soon the clearing was a mass of gyrating bodies. This helped keep the troupe upright as there was no room to fall over.

Keith edged his way out and leant against a tree. This was how it should be at the tenement. Draw everybody in. Get them involved. Then Andre could strike. At least he hoped it would be Andre. The young chef was still working hard on his limp. Everybody had been sounded out for the task. The Reverend Pottie would have liked to have done it. But as he pointed out, the bible clearly stated Thou Shall Not Steal. Trish too, had too reluctantly declined. If she entered the flat uninvited and a man was there, he might get the wrong idea. She felt she still had a certain allure.

And so it went on. The only one to genuinely volunteer, was Sid. But it would take him so long to make the climb, they would be dancing for hours. The engineer was left anxiously hoping everything would be all right on the night.

Chapter 17

Frank arrived to explain the latest legal position. Now the remains were not Duane's, he was confident Lola wouldn't be charged with desecrating a grave. All she had done was remove an intruder from it. Well, part of him.

Keith felt a surge of relief. So he too was in the clear? Not quite, came the reply. Neither of them were.

The engineer grimaced. "What else have we done?"

"Helped a criminal escape from the country. Lola sent him to you for safe keeping."

"But he's dead."

"I know, but he is wanted dead or alive."

His listener put his hand to his brow but said nothing. The lawyer laid a reassuring hand on his knee. "A case of mistaken identity. That will be our defence. You could not have known it was Vincent and neither could Lola. But it may never come to court. I hear you are trying to regain his skull. If you can hand that in with the rest of his bones which you already have, then both your troubles are over. It will be a great day for me."

Keith felt a sudden warmth towards his visitor. "So you celebrate you clients' victories?"

"No, with the reward, Lola can pay all my fee in cash at once. She is threatening to pay me in bananas."

His companion always looked cool in his suit and tie. Yet the mention of money brought perspiration to his brow. The Englishman felt a wave of sympathy. Nobody would ever be able to eat that many. Yet he knew that he too, would be presented with a bill. If only he could pay with fruit from his orchard at home. His funds were dwindling which was another reason why the reward had to be claimed.

The day of the show was fast approaching. The troupe had undertaken their final rehearsal and were now just waiting to recover from its after effects.

Chapter 18

Pistol Shot Rocco sat behind the desk in the small room that served as his office. It was stiflingly hot on the third floor of the tenement. A large fan rotated slowly above his head. He was a bulldog of a man with a short neck and a square, brutal face. Sitting beside his elbow, perfectly polished, was the skull. Rocco had taken over on Vincent's death. But now the leader's head was back, it was exerting considerable influence. Or it certainly seemed that way. Rocco was a born second in command. He had risen to his eminent position because he was bigger and nastier than the others. He would do nothing without consulting the skull. Admittedly guessing its answer was not easy. Yet it did appear to give certain looks if you stared at it long enough. But that made him feel uncomfortable. He might be rough and ready, but knew staring at someone intently from close range was bad manners. Yet after much agonising, he felt his old boss would understand.

Pistol Shot's expression was grave. He was in a dilemma. Should Vincent the Knife be handed in? He called him by his full name out of respect. The gang wanted the reward, but would they be deserting him doing this? The consensus was 'no'. Now he was dead, did it really matter where he ended up? Yet Rocco could not be sure. And what about the rest of him? They would have to dig that up too. They had only just discovered where his bones where and that these increased the reward. Paula had told Stella the girlfriend of his deputy Puncher John.

After a final session with the skull, Pistol Shot gave the go ahead. There had been an imperceptible nod. Once a decision was made, he became decisive. The rest of the skeleton would be dug up that night. There would be room for it on the shelf below the head. It would be nice to have the leader in one piece again. Well two pieces, but close enough together. Then they would think of the best way of turning him in.

The reward would be divided evenly, giving everybody a hefty sum. Each member had already decided what to spend theirs on. Rocco coveted twin gold bracelets in the window of a city centre jewellers. He had earlier tried to obtain them outside shopping hours, but the hammer bounced off the reinforced glass and landed on his foot. He told the hospital a camel had trodden on it. Nobody called him limp-along to his face, but there had been a few sniggers from the gang.

Now fit again, he would be the first to stick a pick into the grave. Once the earth was loosened, his digging team would take over. They liked to sing while they worked, but were strictly forbidden to in the middle of the night. The sleeping villagers must not be disturbed. The thieves hoped to do the job in less than fifteen minutes. There should be nothing to it. After all, they had snatched the head without a soul hearing a sound.

The other members of the team were Puncher John, Bruno, and Henry the Spade who was the gang's corpse burier. He would find it strange digging one up. Sampson should have gone, but had a nasty cough which might waken people.

Pistol Shot wrapped his pick in a large sack that would later contain the skeleton. They had to work as quickly as possible but there must be no snatching. Otherwise Vincent The Knife might disintegrate. Even a missing finger could affect the payout.

A full moon shone as they made their way towards the village. They had left their Mercedes where the tarmac road turned into beaten track. They padded silently along it in single file. The jungle threw shadows across their path. These at times took human shape but nobody jumped out at them. No, at this hour, the entire village was asleep. Rocco just managed to suppress a snigger. When it came to being quiet, he had to set the example. He imagined the consternation there would be in the morning. First the head had gone, and now the body. The witch doctor would have to work hard to protect the rest of the cemetery. But he would be wasting his time. Their job would be done. He began picturing the chunky gold bracelets on his wrists. He always drove with the windows up for security. Now he would wind one down to dangle an arm.

Their destination loomed in the darkness ahead. There was no need to search for the shrine after their last visit. The intruders made their way unerringly to it. Standing like statues, they listened for the slightest sound. There was none. Pistol Shot raised his pick and brought it down with full force. The spade carriers came forward as he stepped back. Five minutes of steady work would cut the earth up. It was a slick operation. Mopping his brow, he watched from behind the nearest tree. It would be his duty to lead the retreat if they were disturbed.

The pile of soil beside the grave grew steadily. The coffin finally came into view and its lid lifted. There was nothing inside. The diggers stared in disbelief and checked their bearings. It was definitely the right spot. Bruno and Henry hurried to give Rocco the bad news. Puncher, in a state of shock, remained silhouetted against the sky The cooking ladle came down on his head with a resounding whack!

"You bastard Duane," shouted Lola. She'd expected her husband to creep back, and unable to sleep, spotted what she thought was a familiar figure. "You bad, bad boy," she cried hitting the figure another sharp blow.

"I'm not Duane," shouted the victim. "I'm Puncher John."

His attacker appearing not to hear, raised her weapon again. But when she brought it down the apparition had gone. The sound of pounding feet came from the forest. These rapidly receded until only Lola's heavy breathing was heard. Then a commotion broke out. Her cries had roused those in the nearest huts who came running. They surrounded the agitated assailant who was muttering to herself. "I was sure it was Duane. I really was."

Ibi looked at the empty coffin. "They were after the skeleton. We removed it just in time."

"We certainly did," agreed Keith, appearing at his elbow. "But we'll have to guard it closely. They'll be back."

"It must be Vincent the Knife's gang."

"Yes, it couldn't be anybody else."

"One of them was called Puncher John," revealed Lola.

"Duane will know their identities," replied the engineer. "So that gives us a vital clue."

And that was what Rocco feared. "What did you give your name for?" he demanded as the fugitives halted with the village safely behind them. "You could have called yourself anything."

"I couldn't help it," replied Puncher. "It just came out."

"You should think more quickly,"

"You can't when you're being bashed around the head. I only said it because she called me Duane."

The darkness hid Pistol Shot's frown. "Duane?" He looked round. "Do any of you know a Duane?"

The onlookers shook their heads, not realising they couldn't be seen. Rocco repeated the question angrily.

96

"No," they chorused.

"Neither do I, but we'll make inquiries."

The chastened group regained the Mercedes and drove off slowly. There was no triumphant squealing of tyres. Pistol Shot in the driving seat, sighed with frustration. There would be no chunky gold bracelets just yet. His wrists were beginning to feel naked.

Chapter 19

Keith, in his room at the rear of Lola's hut, couldn't get back to sleep. With the skeleton missing, the gang would realise the village knew its value. So they would guard the head ever more closely. As the village would the body. It would be no good if either regained one part but lost the other. It was like a jig saw, you had to have every piece. The question was, did the gang know about the English party? The engineer could only keep his fingers crossed they didn't. It was lucky their dancing display was coming quickly.

On the drive home it had indeed dawned on Rocco that if the villagers had removed the skeleton, they must know the skull's identity. And therefore its value. And they would be coming after it. Or would they? His eyes narrowed. They were just harmless country people. If they discovered it was Vincent the Knife's gang, the name itself would put sheer terror into them. The gang would return in broad daylight, and armed. The inhabitants would quickly hand over the prize. A confident smile spread across his brutal features. Yes, it would be one way traffic. A fitting metaphor, he thought, as the car sped through the deserted streets.

When the English party arrived in the morning, Keith broke the news. There was immediate consternation. Vincent the Knife was scaring enough, but now there was Puncher John.

"Maybe it's Punched John," said Andre hopefully. He was still favourite for the dangerous mission.

"Lola is adamant it is Puncher," said the engineer, "He presented her with an easy target so he must be big."

An aura of doom spread over the company. If two of the gang had reputations for knifing and punching,

98

what did the others have? It was one thing planning to fool a faceless mob, but quite another when their ruthless characteristics began to appear. Only now did the incredible seriousness of the situation begin to sink in.

Keith knew it was only fair to give everyone a last chance to change their mind. He called for silence and said if anyone wanted to drop out, they should take one step forward. Several feet shuffled in the dust but nobody did. He felt a surge of gratitude and admiration. Yet if the truth be known there were many faint hearts. But the fear of embarrassment at being thought a coward, just outweighed the dangers of going on.

With the die cast, shoulders were straightened and chins raised. Keith could only hope the mood would not evaporate before the show. The party decided to return to their hotel until the time came to set out for their ordeal. In the meantime the skeleton would be hidden in a tree. The gang would never think of looking there if they returned to search the huts.

Chapter 20

On the outskirts of the city, Rocco was marshalling his forces for the raid on the village. They had decided to act before lunch so they would be back for the show that evening. The six members would travel in three cars. They could have fitted into two, but it made the convoy look longer. They were dressed in black track suits that matched their designer shades. Pistol Shot had issued instructions these must be removed when searching the huts for they restricted vision. This caused dismay among the fashion conscious, but they saw his point. They carried guns, knives and silver knuckle dusters. Rocco also had a hand grenade. It looked impressive dangling from his belt.

They high fived each other before leaping into their vehicles and roaring off. Pistol Shot led with Puncher John while Bruno and Sampson followed ahead of Marvin and Stiletto Rod. Raymond remained with a machete to guard the skull. He put it in a tin box and sat on it.

Reaching the village, the convoy drew up in a cloud of dust in the clearing. It was an intimidating arrival. Particularly by Stiletto Rod and Marvin who ran over a chicken. Ibi watched from the shade of a mango tree. He had been expecting such a visit and the village was prepared. City dwellers saw them as ignorant peasants and that is exactly what they would be.

Rocco got out and removing his dark glasses, gave them a polish. It would allow the inhabitants hovering in their huts, a chance to see his brutal looks. He narrowed his eyes against the sun which heightened the effect. The head man stepped forward, his face by contrast, showing a disarming smile.

"Welcome brothers."

Pistol Shot fingered his grenade. "Where's the skeleton?"

"We have many of them. They are all in our burial ground." He paused. "Except one."

Rocco raised his eyebrows. "Yes?"

"It's missing. It's head went first, then the body. An evil spirit took them. It appeared in human form. One of our women hit it with a cooking ladle and it ran off. It was not a brave spirit."

His listener cast an angry glance at Puncher John.

"But it was clever" continued the headman. "It crept back and took its prize while we were not looking."

A hint of suspicion entered Rocco's voice. "How do you know it came back?"

"There can be no other explanation. In the morning the skeleton was gone."

"So nobody saw anything?"

"No. we were too frightened to keep watch."

"Maybe one of your villagers took it?"

"Why?"

"To get a reward."

Ibi managed a genuine look of amazement. "Reward? What reward?"

His interrogator ignored the question. "I think we'll take a look around."

"Are you from the government?"

"Of course - the cemetery department. There's been a lot of grave robbing." He waved an arm and his men spread out to begin their search. The occupants of the huts under strict orders from Ibi, stood passively by. Not a nook or cranny was left untouched. Pistol Shot stood watching in the shade of a nearby tree, unaware the object he sought was dangling above his head. Ibi prayed he would not look up. The foliage was thick, but he noticed too late a foot had been left carelessly in

101

view.

Yet Rocco was only intent on what was happening in front of him. And his frustration grew as each hut was found to be empty. Did the villagers know anything? Were they trying to pull banana skins over his eyes? He studied the figure standing beside him. The head man wore his most vacant expression. He knew he must not overdo it. Although his mouth was open, he refrained from dribbling.

At last the search was finished. The men stood round their boss with crestfallen faces. They had looked everywhere. Rocco's face darkened. What to do next? He could put a gun to the head man's head but he seemed to know nothing. Yet if that was true, who had taken the skeleton? Were there others after it? It was too hot to think. He got into his car and turned on the air conditioning. The others did the same. They sat there with the engines running. Ibi sidled up to Patu. "Are they leaving?"

"No, they're thinking. They're cooler inside."

"Can you put a spell on them?"

"It's difficult through tinted glass."

"They are not government officials?"

"No, they are the criminals who came in the night. They do not know how much we know. They are deciding whether to use violence. They have several choices of weapon."

Ibi felt the beads of sweat on his brow grow bigger. Was he going to have his brains blown out? The witch doctor was quick to reassure him. That would not be so. They were much more likely to use a knife.

Rocco in turn felt his blood pressure rising. He wished the skull was there to give him a few hints. Vincent would know what to do. Under stress, Pistol Shot tended to forget his former boss's full title. He had

102

thought of bringing him along. But it would have been awkward. Puncher liked to sit in the front and to put the head in the back would have been disrespectful. For one thing, it might roll about. Puncher was sure Ibi knew where the skeleton was. He wanted to stake him out in the path of marching ants. The trouble was, there weren't any about. Or they could tie him to a palm tree and pelt him with coconuts. Pistol Shot was inclined to adopt the carrot and the stick approach. Puncher should live up to his name and knock his teeth out. Then if he came clean, they'd be replaced with gold ones. Nothing could be fairer than that. But of course life wasn't fair. Rocco had learnt that when the hammer bounced back from the window. It made him think of the injury. If he had to kick the head man, he would use the other foot.

Puncher became restless and Rocco realised the others would be too. If only he could consult his old boss. He tried mental telepathy to no avail. He wondered if Raymond, sitting on the box was impeding his signal. He considered calling him on his mobile to lift the lid, but felt it would make no difference.

After more agonised thought, he decided what to do. He would live up to his name. He would take a pistol in each hand and menacingly approach the head man. Sudden confrontations produced startled looks which would betray innocence or guilt. If Ibi showed the slightest shiftiness, he would whack him over the head and drag him off to a hut for interrogation.

He emerged into the midday sun. The weapons glinting in his hands. He strode towards the tree where Ibi had been standing. He was not there. Rocco toured all points of the compass. But whatever direction he took, the head man was nowhere to be seen. Neither was anybody else. The village was deserted. Everybody had fled into the jungle. The thwarted hunter cursed the

103

vehicles' tinted windows. He had noticed nothing, and neither had the rest of the gang. Away from his gaze, they'd tuned into their radios and were thumping on the dashboards to the music. He ordered them out to search the surrounding undergrowth. Yet he knew it was a hopeless task. Soon they were summoned back. Instead they would play a waiting game. The fugitives couldn't stay away for ever. And when they returned, there would be a big reckoning. By vanishing, they had proved their guilt. There would be no mercy now. If Ibi lost his teeth, there would be no replacements. If he had to live on soft fruit so be it. That is, if he was to be left alive. The honour of the gang was at stake. If this debacle got out, they would lose a lot of face. He would not be Pistol Shot Rocco, but Pistol Clot Rocco. He shuddered. That must never happen. Even if he had to beat up every villager. Except of course those under eight. He did not want a reputation as a bully.

The sun moved remorselessly across the sky. Rocco stubbed his tenth cigarette into an overflowing ash tray. Puncher beside him, chewed gum silently. He had given up smoking four weeks ago and was finding it an ordeal. There was a knock on the window. It was Stiletto Rod. How much longer were they going to wait? The leader felt a flash of anger. It was the same question Sampson had asked ten minutes earlier. And he had been told to pass on the answer. They were staying until the villagers appeared. Stiletto plucked up courage. "What about the show?"

Rocco tried to hide his impatience. "What about what show?"

"The foreign dance troupe. You promised we could watch it. That's why we came early."

A note of menace crept into Rocco's voice "The situation has changed."

"But you promised man, we want to go home."

It hardened even further. "Is this a mutiny?"

"No boss, but we're restless. We're sitting here looking at nothing. The villagers could be gone for days."

"Don't be so sure. There could be a hundred pairs of eyes on us."

"We've had a good look round. They are not here."

"Go back to your car."

He watched the retreating figure with a steely glare.

"Puncher, collect the ignition keys. We don't want anybody disappearing."

The second in command did as he was told, glad to get away from the smoke. He returned to place them on the dashboard. "Marvin said to ask you a question"

"What is it?"

"When are we going home?"

Rocco felt he was going to explode.

"Not you two as well?

"We could return after the show. Nothing would be lost. And we'd have our minds fully on the job. At the moment, the boys are thinking of nothing but the dance. The posters make it look good."

Pistol Shot rubbed his chin pensively. He secretly agreed. The Lambeth Walk for a start, intrigued him. Maybe the gang could adopt it as one of their rituals. High fiving had become boring however enthusiastic they tried to be. He could also see that just by sitting there, the gang conceded the initiative. That made up his mind. He was not heartless when it came to looking after his men. They would see the show, and then return in the dead of night to catch the villagers in their beds.

But he would make sure no one joined in the revelry. Especially Sampson and Bruno. They would be completely useless on the second raid if they were 'danced out.'

The ignition keys were returned and the convey edged discreetly out of the clearing. Rocco looked on the bright side. It had not been a wasted journey. The villagers knew of the skeleton and its value. Otherwise they would not have fled. But would they be brave enough to try to get the skull? No. Somebody would have to do it for them. But who? One thing was sure, Vincent would be well guarded. He tut tutted. He had done it again. Vincent the Knife, he corrected himself. It was all a matter of respect. He hoped when he died his skull would be treated the same way. He cast a furtive glance at his deputy. Somehow, he felt it wouldn't. He would demote Puncher when their latest member had settled in. He had high hopes of Cranium Crusher Jones. He was tough and strong, but as yet untried. That's why he'd been left behind on the raid.

Rocco was careful over accepting recruits. There were a lot of police informers about. Yet Crusher seemed a natural criminal. When they went shoplifting, things just stuck to his fingers. And he had made himself indispensable. He opened Pistol Shot's cans of Coca Cola and polished his sun glasses. He used a special duster with the word BOSS written on it. Rocco liked that. It denoted respect. He felt if the worst happened, the newcomer would treat his skull in the same way. He looked contemptuously at Puncher who was chewing steadily. At least Crusher wouldn't run away from a woman with a cooking ladle.

The cars drew up outside the tenement building. The latest recruit was patrolling a space big enough for each vehicle. A succession of cowed motorists had been moved on. Rocco whistled softly in admiration. Yes, a deputy in the making. He would take him on the raid later that night and give him a free hand. Why not let him loose? He was the type to stand no nonsense. If nothing else, he would galvanise the others.

But first things first. Was the skull still safe? He strode up to the third floor and flung open the door. Raymond was still sitting on the box clutching his machete. No, he had not moved. Rocco lifted the head out reverently and returned it to the top of his desk. It would have to go back for the show but deserved some fresh air.

Chapter 21

Keith and Belinda sat in the foyer watching the others descending the stairs. They had left their room first, finding it impossible to rest. Their stomachs were full of butterflies. They could not have been more nervous if they'd been making their debuts in the West End. From their strained faces, the rest of the troupe were obviously feeling the same. It was one thing to put on a show in a friendly village. Quite another to do it in a run down part of the city surrounded by violent characters. And while trying to steal a human skull at the same time.

The engineer worried their dismal expressions would create the wrong atmosphere. He ordered everybody to start practicing fixed smiles. Reggie was the only natural at this, being a publican. Andre had given up limping. He knew he was the only real candidate for the snatch, and was resigned to his fate. He thought of himself as Gary Cooper in High Noon. A man had to do, what a man had to do. Yet he had only seen the black and white film once long ago. And then he had snogged his girlfriend all the way through until the shoot out at the end.

The Reverend Pottie's knees were aching and he hoped they would recover in time. He had been on them for an hour telling God the Ten Commandments should be more flexible. If they got the head, they would be breaching Thou Shalt Not Steal. Yet the reward would give the villagers a better way of life. Surely that was preferable? He had concentrated hard, but was still waiting for a reply.

Trish had dropped off fitfully, dreaming her pet had been shot and made into a pie. She took this as a bad omen. Tom and Rita had passed the time blancoing each other's tennis shoes. It would help them stand out as the best dancers which they considered themselves to be. Sid came down with Joyce's instructions to keep in step, ringing in his ears. He knew he was the weakest link but as he told her, if he was meant to be a chorus girl, he would have been born a woman.

Reggie was the only one who had slept soundly, and he'd had a wonderful dream. He was much taken by the breasts of the young girls in the village, and had been recruiting topless barmaids for his pub. He couldn't bear to turn anybody down until Keith had pointed out there would be no room for customers.

The troupe boarded their coach. The engineer undertook a roll call. He knew they were all there, but wanted to see if there were any nervous replies. Then if anybody needed counselling, they could have a one to one chat. Nobody did. They had got over their fears. There was an air of confidence, although this became brittle as the scenery changed. The tarmac roads gave way to pot holes and the buildings became ramshackle. The city centre was far behind when they entered a narrow street which ended in a small square. It was hemmed in on all sides by tall tenements. This was to be their dance floor. Somebody had attempted to sweep it, but two empty beer cans rolled around in the breeze. Posters for the show were stuck on several walls. They were attractive and colourful. Trish had done a good job. Now they would have to live up to them. They disembarked with flushed faces. A bottle had been passed round as their preparations got off to an early start.

Keith shielded his eyes against the sun. It was beginning to fade, but still bright. A row of sunglasses appeared to march towards him. Pistol Shot, as the prominent figure in the neighbourhood, led the welcoming committee. He took the engineer's hand in his huge fist and introduced the gang members. The only two missing were Raymond, who was sitting on the skull, and Cranium Crusher Jones who had been taking him a drink of pineapple.

Crusher now came strolling into view. Rocco was standing slightly apart from the crowd with Keith and beckoned him over. The respective leaders were already on good terms with Pistol Shot calling his guest Keithy for extra intimacy. This sally made its recipient wince, but it was nothing to the one he produced on seeing the new arrival.

"Our latest recruit," said Rocco. "Cranium Crusher Jones."

He was then called away to organise another sweeping of the square. Keith looked at the figure before him and slowly began to shake his head. "Duane, Duane, what are you doing?"

"I've infiltrated."

"But you know anything you touch is a total disaster."

"You need somebody on the inside."

"That's where we'll end up, or underground."

His friend's voice sounded confident. "But they don't suspect anything."

"That ridiculous name. How did you get that?"

"I couldn't be Ping Pong Pete or Handshake Harry could I? Not in a gang led by Pistol Shot Rocco and Puncher John. I've got to play a part."

You've played enough parts already."

"This is the most vital. I'll be able to get the skull during the show."

"How are you going to do that?"

"I don't know."

Keith's brow clouded. "You don't know?"

"I don't know yet. I've still got two hours."

"You'll have to be a fast thinker."

His co-conspirator waved a hand for silence. "I'm concentrating now."

The engineer closed his eyes and muttered a prayer. Somehow he did not believe it would do any good. "If you want help you must tell us quickly," he warned. "Once we start dancing it'll be too late."

His listener nodded absentmindedly. Keith stifled a sigh, and went to rejoin the troupe. When Duane was in a trance, it was like talking to a brick wall. For the moment, they would stick to their original plan. Andre would sneak up to the third floor at the height of the show. He hoped it would not conflict with anything Duane might come up with. Yet the risk had to be taken. Anything was better than inaction.

The sides of the square started to fill. The expectant crowd was arriving early. Faces began appearing at the windows above. Keith worked out the one the skull was thought to be in. There was nobody there. Was it kept empty and locked? He imagined Andre's shoulder charge splintering the door. No, it would not be that simple.

The troupe began to get ready. They were given a room on the ground floor of the gang's tenement. Sid was massaging his legs. Each muscle needed to be woken up individually. The young chef was shadow boxing. Presumably preparing for his coming escapade rather than the Hokey Cokey. Rita was fiddling with the bra Tom insisted on her wearing. Earlier she had done without, feeling freer, but he said it made her too bouncy.

The vicar was deciding whether to wear his clerical collar. It highlighted his occupation if anybody wanted to discuss Christianity. Yet it rubbed raw when the sweat began to flow and he couldn't look down to see what his feet were doing. In the end he decided against it.

When the dancers took to the square, they found the crowd had grown enormously. There wasn't a spare place to be seen. Several boys were sitting in the branches of a tree in the middle of the square. Trish and Rita made a mental note not to perform under it. They didn't want the youths peering down their fronts. A sound system had been set up and Rocco took the microphone. He was sporting a pink shirt and matching baseball cap. "The square is going to shake man," he shrieked. "With Keithy's gang. They're oldies but goodies - not no good hoodies."

This brought a roar of approval from the enthralled throng. Reggie gave his trousers a final hitch and looked around. He wondered how many he would let into his pub. There couldn't be more than half a dozen without a criminal record. And then only because they hadn't been caught. Talk about being in the lion's den. But to be fair, they weren't innocents themselves. They were taking advantage of wonderful hospitality in order to steal a skull. Well, hopefully. But then what? How would they get out? There must be a dozen machetes to the yard, never mind the guns. He'd prefer to be shot rather than chopped up. Not that he'd get a choice. He determinedly pushed such thoughts away. He needed a cheerful face and these weren't helping.

Fixed grins were appearing among the troupe. The din was so loud, he couldn't tell whether Trish was talking or her teeth were chattering. She looked pale despite the heat. The sun was almost down, but the enclosed square showed no signs of becoming cooler. Pistol Shot was introducing each member of the troupe to the crowd. The landlord wished he'd been A. N.

Other, but it was too late. The roll call finished, the master of ceremonies gave a final whoop and relinquished the microphone.

The Niger Stomp had been moved to the finale slot. Whenever it was done first, the audience joined in and you couldn't get them off. As Sid said, you'd need a cowboy with a lasso. The dancers took up their positions, and at a sign from Keith, launched into the Lambeth Walk. Rita quickly found her bra restricting, but had to grin and bear it. The vicar as always, was finding it difficult to throw himself into his role and remain dignified. In the heat of the moment, he could never tell his left from his right. This was awkward when you had to throw yourself about. The engineer was going through the motions, but his mind was elsewhere. He kept glancing up at the third floor window which remained unattended. Duane had said earlier the skull was definitely there in a box. Maybe it had been moved? No, it would be better protected in the gang's headquarters. He looked at Rocco who sat on a bench at the front with his followers. His top of the range trainers were tapping in time with the beat. The gang seemed to be enjoying themselves. As were the raucous crowd. There was a carnival atmosphere. Things could not be going better. Soon Andre would detach himself and begin his climb.

Raymond sat on his box, a forlorn figure. He had asked if he could drag it to the window to watch, but his leader had said no. It would be too distracting, He had to be fully alert at all times. It was a great honour to guard Vincent The Knife rather than watch a boring dance. He stiffened as the door opened, but it was only Cranium Crusher Jones bringing him another drink. This time it was his favourite mango juice and slid sweetly down. His visitor watched him keenly. He had taken a leaf out of Andre's book and popped something special into the glass. It would work much more quickly than in a shepherd's pie. And when it did, he would be on hand to offer to guard the box.

The perpetrator did not have long to wait. His victim, first wearing a thoughtful, and then agonised expression, became increasingly agitated. He began squirming as if reorganising the cheeks of his bottom. Duane found it hard to hide a grin. His plan was working perfectly. Finally the distracted Raymond leapt up, opened the box and yanked out the head.

"What are you doing?" asked the startled infiltrator.

"I'm going to the john, man."

"You can't take Vincent with you."

"No time to talk," cried the distraught guard, and ran from the room. Duane followed him down the passage as the lavatory door slammed shut. His pursuer stood outside. "You can't take Vincent in there, it's disrespectful."

"Vincent the Knife."

"OK, Vincent The Knife, Vincent The Fork. It doesn't matter what he's called," retorted Duane beginning to lose his temper. "It's horrible to make him watch what you're doing."

An indignant reply floated towards him. "Don't you dare call him Vincent The Fork."

Duane fought to keep calm. "Sorry. But you will not be a nice sight."

"I've turned his face to the wall."

"He can hear you."

"Don't be silly man, he's only a skull."

"Then why is it so important to guard him?"

"He's still our leader, ask Rocco."

"And you know what he's like when he gets upset."

"When who gets upset?

114

"Both of them. Pistol Shot will be just as angry as Vincent The Knife."

"I gave an oath I wouldn't let him out of my sight."

"But you didn't expect to be sitting on the john."

"No, I went twice this morning."

"Neither of them will take that as an excuse."

There was silence. Duane could almost hear the incarcerated one thinking. The voice that came through the door had a slight quaver. "Vincent The Knife had to go to the john when he was alive. He will understand."

"But he didn't take anybody with him."

"He was not in my situation. He didn't guard skulls, he cracked them."

Duane felt his frustration rising. He fought to control himself. Time was running out. "Well, we don't want to get ours cracked do we?"

"Why would they crack yours?"

"Because I didn't take over guard duty and let you take Vinny to the john."

"Vincent the Knife."

"O.K. Vincent the Knife. But they'll hit you the hardest." The speaker thought he heard an intake of breath. At that moment, there came a noise from the other end of the corridor. Should he investigate? No, he had to keep the pressure on Raymond.

Andre had entered the office, panting. He had held his breath while climbing three flights of stairs. It was empty and the box lay unattended in the middle of the floor. He wanted to pinch himself to see if he was dreaming, but did not have time. He picked it up, and holding it to his chest, ran back down as fast as he could. Keith, who had detached himself from the dancers, waited in the shadow of the hall. Outside, the onlookers still watched, entranced. Thrusting his load into the engineer's arms, the young chef punched the air in delight like a goal scoring footballer.

Keith put the box down and calmly opened it. "You twat, it's empty."

The would be thief scratched his head. "I thought it was light, but I didn't think Skulky weighed that much."

The engineer winced once again at the nick name, but let the matter pass. This was no time for small talk. "Get the box back upstairs before anybody finds it's missing. Then have a good look round. Vincent could have been put in a cupboard or on top of a shelf."

"They wouldn't just leave him lying about."

"They're not expecting a raid are they?"

"I flipping hope not." The young chef picked up the box and set off for the third floor. Again he met nobody. The office was still empty, but he heard footsteps coming along the corridor towards him. A figure appeared in the doorway.

"Duane," Andre gasped.

"Andre," said Duane, looking quizzically at the newcomer holding the box.

"I was seeing if there was anything in it," came the rather shamefaced reply as he hastily put it down.

"The skull's in the john," revealed his companion.

The young chef's eyes widened. "What? Have they hidden it in the cistern?"

"No, it's on the guard's lap."

Duane quickly outlined the situation. Andre looked out of the window. He could see the troupe were into their final dance. It was now or never, and there was not a moment to lose. Squaring his shoulders, he almost ran past a startled Duane who hastened in his wake. Picking up speed as he went, Andre crashed into the door that barred him from his prize. It splintered at the hinges and fell inwards on top of the helpless

116

Raymond. The skull fell to the floor and rolled towards the intruder who scooped it up. He threw it to Duane who caught it neatly and headed for the stairs.

Throwing off the door, Raymond lunged at Andre who was also taking to his heels. The enraged victim was gaining dangerously on the young chef when nature abruptly called again. Skidding to a halt, he managed a desperate about-turn to regain his sanctuary with a second to spare. Duane reached the hallway just ahead of his fellow intruder who had taken the stairs four at a time. Keith was waiting anxiously at the foot. Taking the skull, he shoved it in Andre's bag noting it was from a downtown supermarket. Hardly Harrods or John Lewis, but Vincent didn't deserve one of quality. Flanked by the two burglars, he hurried to the coach. The last dance was finishing and the audience was joining in.

One by one, the troupe extracted themselves from the heaving mass. Perspiring freely, they slumped into their seats. The engineer almost pulled them aboard in his desperation to get quickly away. But one place remained empty. Trish was still flinging herself about in the middle of the crowd. Her eyes were glazed, and her head bobbed up and down rhythmically in time with her knees.

"She's gone," said Rita knowledgeably. "The beat's got her, it does that."

"Well, she's got to be ungot," declared Keith. "Every second we stay here increases the danger."

"She won't stop until the music does."

"But that will go on all night."

"What are we going to do?" asked Joyce, fighting down a feeling of panic.

"We can't leave," said the vicar. "They'll take her hostage if they find out what we have been up to."

"She won't notice, the state she's in," said Andre.

"Somebody's got to go and get her," said Belinda. "And right now."

"I'll go," volunteered Tom. "I won't talk to her. I'll just take her hands and we'll twirl our way out."

"You can't do a waltz in that throng," ventured Reggie. "Not with everybody stamping their feet."

"No, it'll be more of a quick step."

"It needs to be very quick indeed," said the young chef.

Tom needed no urging. Like the rest, he knew the folly of hanging about. He edged his way through the sweating bodies to the side of the entranced figure. As he reached out, her partner picked her up and swung her round and round. Each time she passed Tom, her face became paler. Oh no, he thought, she's going to be sick. On the ground again she was left swaying with her eyes closed. He caught her as her legs gave way. Dancing was definitely out. He couldn't drag her, so there was only one thing for it. The fireman's chair. Carefully avoiding the pumping elbows around him, he hoisted her over his shoulders and pushed his way through to the coach. He was met by a burst of enthusiastic applause as he tipped the limp figure into her seat.

Soon the bus was speeding down near empty streets. Keith couldn't help inspecting Duane's head which was now Vincent's. He would have to get used to its new identity. As would everybody else. It would not be easy having been Duane's for so long. The real Duane sat beside him, having left another of his identities behind.

When the theft was discovered, Cranium Crusher Jones was nowhere to be found. This was just as well. Rocco was in a towering rage. Suddenly the gold bracelets were further away than ever. He had stopped

118

in mid dance, stirred by compassion. Raymond was missing all the fun. He must be relieved. Pistol Shot found Marvin and escorted him upstairs to ensure a proper handover. The replacement was upset at leaving the celebrations, but his leader had patted him on the head and said there was no reason why he couldn't tap his feet and snap his fingers while sitting on the box.

The office was empty, as was Vincent's hiding place which lay with its lid open. From down the passage came the sound of what can best be described as earnest endeavour. The pair headed towards it and stopped short. Rocco knew the expression caught with your trousers down. But had never seen it portrayed to such effect before. The hapless figure sat open to the world. The shattered door lay beside him. He always stood up before the boss. It was a mark of respect. But under the circumstances, it was impossible. He remained glued to his seat.

Rocco fought to contain himself. "Where is Vincent The Knife?"

His voice was even but full of menace. His eyes were mere slits. Raymond shuddered. The effect on him would have been calamitous if he had not been in that condition already. He opened his mouth but no words came out. He tried again and produced one. "Gone."

His interrogator's next question was edged with ice. "Where?"

Raymond found himself shrugging his shoulders. "I don't know." Slowly and painfully he told what had happened. Pistol Shot's eyes continued to narrow until twice they ended up shut. The forlorn figure in front of him hoped he'd fallen asleep. But it was anything but the case. His mind was whirling. Who really was Cranium Crusher Jones? And what had he been talking to the Englishman about? They were clearly working together. And they must be connected to the village. A stab of pain hit his forehead. His brain was only used to working in short bursts. But he had to soldier on. If one foreigner was involved then they all were. And why had they rushed off without saying goodbye? His farewell speech on several sheets of A4 was burning a hole in his pocket. He would leave them for Raymond. It looked as if they could well be needed. Obviously something had been popped into his drink. Something very effective indeed. He must find out what it was and make a note of it.

He glanced at the victim with the tiniest hint of pity. What would he have done in the circumstances? He liked to be fair before he killed someone. Would he have made a dash for it and left the skull behind? Raymond deserved credit for taking it with him. Maybe he would only shoot him in the leg. He had also refused to hand it over when cornered. And he had then tried to pursue the thieves when nature so cruelly intervened.

Rocco was the first to acknowledge that you couldn't answer it and run at the same time. He remembered Pedro having an accident when the police suddenly appeared during a store robbery. He was the only one that was caught.

He decided to wrap up the interview. Raymond's mind was on other things and there was no time to be lost. The English troupe must be tracked down and Vincent The Knife recovered before he could be reunited with his skeleton. Pistol Shot feared that too, was in their possession. The reward was slipping away. It called for desperate measures. He would call a meeting first thing in the morning. But now he had to stop the dancing. To be at your murderous best, you needed at least six hours sleep. Every member of the

120

gang must be ultra fresh for the battle ahead.

Chapter 22

The stars were fading when Rocco went round dousing everybody with buckets of iced water. They had had their allotted time. Yet he had been unable to sleep a wink. They would have to do the fighting while he did the organising. Unless he could get his hands on an English neck. The way he was feeling, he would throttle it even if it's owner was already dead.

There was a hundred percent turn out. Nobody wanted to miss the fun. Raymond looked wan, and appeared to have lost weight, but was bent on revenge. They sat in rows on the edge of the square. Thirty heads riveted to the figure striding up and down before them. Pistol Shot could not keep still. If he stopped, he shook with rage. He had spent the night preparing his talk and outlining tactics and targets. But as soon as he started speaking, he forgot it. Anger took over.

"The English like to dance eh? We will make them dance. Bullets will bounce at their feet. Then when they are dancing, we will lift our guns higher. And - ."

Puncher John felt he had to intervene. Things were getting out of hand with less than a minute gone. "You can't go machine gunning a bunch of foreign tourists."

"Tourists?" Rocco's eyes blazed. "Not tourists. Raiders, thieves, invaders. They have stolen Vincent The Knife. We must get him back and take our revenge." The speaker glared at his second in command. "We have no room for chicken hearts."

Puncher felt his indignation rising but stayed calm. There was no point in adding fuel to the flames. "I want what everybody wants. I want them dead."

Pistol Shot brightened. "Is that true?" he asked loudly. A forest of hands shot up. He nodded contentedly. That was one factor decided.

"What I meant," Puncher emphasised. "Is that the job must be done professionally. No remains, no investigation. Just nine slit throats and a crocodile dinner party."

Rocco frowned. "But there'll be a search if they go missing."

"White men have disappeared in the jungle for centuries. If there are no clues, it will soon peter out."

"That means not taking anything from the bodies," warned the leader. "Sporting dead men's trinkets can get you caught."

Faces among the audience fell. There was nothing like ripping a Rolex off a limp wrist. Or yanking a gold chain from under a sagging chin. Those were the spoils of war. But this was a different war. The war of Vincent The Knife's head. He would not like them putting their own interests first.

Rocco sensed their thoughts. They must be single minded. To get their hands on the skull was their first objective. Whatever stood in their way. And what did? A bunch of pensioners and old women. Once they'd met, it would be over in the flash of a knife. The problem would be finding them.

The eager pursuers were quickly allotted tasks. To check all hotels to discover where the English were staying. And to keep an eye on the village and surrounding ones in case they sought sanctuary there. Each member was thrown a mango. There was no time for breakfast. With their blood up, most were too excited to eat. They fingered their weapons as the waited for the signal to go like runners at a starting tape. They had machine guns, shot guns and pistols. And for those who liked to work at closer quarters, machetes, knives and the odd ball bearing in a sock.

One by one, the cars roared off. Their drivers

negotiating the bumpy surface at top speed. Four of the men travelled more sedately. They had drawn the short straw. There would be no glory for them. Yet Rocco stressed their job was highly important. They were to watch the government office where Vincent The Knife's remains must be delivered to claim the reward. Any suspicious characters with bulky parcels must be checked. He wouldn't put it past Keithy to lead the gang on a wild goose chase while sending someone to sneak in with the prize. There must be no chatting at their posts or flicking through pornography. Their surveillance must be water tight. They would be relieved after eight hours. But by then the gang might well have got the skull back.

Pistol Shot retired to the tenement for a large meal. He did not know when he would be able to eat again. He felt he had all angles covered. Nigeria was large, but the fugitives were conspicuous. And they couldn't go far if they were to deliver Vincent The Knife's remains safely to the authorities. At the thought of his leader, Rocco took out a vivid yellow handkerchief and wiped away a tear. If anybody deserved to rest in peace he did. Especially after a busy life full of robberies and stabbings. Yet what had happened? He'd been chopped up and spread all over the place. True, his boys had got a piece of him back, but had lost it again. Thanks to a nasty underhand trick. So much for the English sense of fair play. A vast bowl of pounded yam appeared. He brightened. This was more like it. The foreigners would find two could play at being dirty.

Chapter 23

As the searchers began their sweep, the troupe were checking out of their hotel. They knew within the hour somebody would be looking at its register. The party headed for the village. Keith realised it would soon be watched, but wanted Ibi's advice. They needed somewhere to hide while they put Vincent's bones together and decided how to deliver them. Then at last they could go home.

The head man was waiting in the clearing. He had despatched sentries into the surrounding bush to warn of approaching strangers. The skeleton had been moved to a secret underground cave and would take time to be recovered. It meant the troupe would have to spend at least one night on the run. But where? They could not stay in a hotel or village. If they did, they ran the risk of being murdered in their beds. That only left the jungle. Yet they had no equipment. Not even a tent or groundsheet. And they feared the wild animals.

Ibi went off to confer with Patu. He returned to tell Keith of the perfect place. The engineer listened gravely and turned to the group. "We'll be up in the air tonight."

A frisson of excitement ran through the onlookers. Were they flying home? Getting out while the going was good?

The engineer spoke slowly and clearly "Ibi says two large trees should take us comfortably."

There was a dumbfounded silence. A startled Reggie was the first to break it. "You mean we'll be sleeping on branches?"

"Yes."

"All nine of us?"

"Yes."

"Me Tarzan," said Andre, thumping his chest.

Rita ignored him. "What happens if we fall off?"

"You won't. We will make sure everybody's secure."

"What about snakes?" asked Joyce.

"They don't like company, they'll go off somewhere else."

"What if they come back?"

"They won't."

"Then what about spiders?"

"The same thing."

"There is nothing to worry about," declared Ibi. "I have asked Patu to put a spell on the trees. Nothing will come near them."

"I hope that includes Rocco," said the publican.

It was too dangerous for the party to remain in the village a moment longer. They spent the day on the banks of a stream well off the beaten path. Meanwhile two of Ibi's men were sent to collect the skeleton. If Rocco brutally tortured any villagers they might reveal its hiding place. Better to keep it up the tree with the skull.

As the sun began to set, the party made their way to their new homes which stood side by side. These towered a hundred feet above them, standing starkly against the sky. Keith and Ibi were anxious to get everybody aloft before darkness fell. And there was another reason for speed. One of the lookouts had spotted a figure lurking in the undergrowth. He was speaking into a purple mobile. Ibi looked grave. There were seven in the village, five black, one silver and one yellow.

The engineer had felt it inevitable they would be found. He took out his own and tapped out a number. Inspector Howard, back in his Devon office answered.

"Hello." His eyebrows shot up. "Keith, you're what? Climbing a tree?" He rubbed his nose. "Special Branch eh? Sorry, no time for jokes. I see, hmmm, sounds serious. Yes, I agree it's worth a try. Good luck." He clicked off and looked round the room. "That Porter fellow's gone native."

Keith and Ibi redoubled their efforts to get everybody moving. Several were jittery. They had no head for heights and it was affecting the others. Rita said every time she looked at her tree it got taller.

"Ladies first," said the Reverend Pottie, trying to be helpful.

"No thank you," retorted Trish. "I don't want you looking up my skirt."

"I'm a man of God," he replied huffily.

"No offence vicar, but they're some of the worst."

"For goodness sake," said Keith. "If we're caught on the ground, we will be massacred."

One by one, the fugitives began to haul themselves up. Ibi sent some of his men aloft with them. They bent and twisted branches to make platforms and back rests. The party were told to move as little as possible although they were plenty of dangling vines to hold onto. It was difficult to relax. Not everybody had faith in Patu's promise to remove all former occupants. The constant rustling did not help. Was it the breeze, or a python slithering along a branch?

Reggie's behind fitted perfectly into the well of his tree. So much so, he worried if he would be able to get out. This is a right caper, he thought to himself. If ever there was a case of 'time gentlemen please,' this was it. He wanted to go home. The long stay car park would be costing him a fortune. There would have to be a whip round. That is if they survived to make it. Would the gang spare the women? He had a sudden idea.

Could he fit into any of their dresses? No, he was not a coward. He would front up to Rocco if anybody would. Yet he couldn't fight the whole gang by himself. There were times when you had to hide your bravery. It was no good being shot for nothing. He paused. Or would he be shot? He could just as easily be knifed or macheted. You never knew what type of weapon these criminals carried. The sensible answer was negotiation. But how could you talk to these people? No, there could be no peaceful outcome. It would be a fight to the death. He sighed, and wedged himself more firmly into his hole.

Tom and Rita, who had shared the same bed every night for forty years, found themselves on separate branches. They had been round and round the tree, but could not find one big enough for two. They had complained to Ibi who was sorry, but said it was unrealistic for them to expect it to provide a double.

Keith was adjusting his back to a smooth expanse of trunk, when a shadowy figure appeared beside him. It was Duane. He had been dropped off in the city centre when they were fleeing from the tenement. He confirmed his worst fears. According to Paula's girlfriend, Rocco's scouts had reported in, and he knew where the foreigners were. To within a tree or two. They would not take long to home in on their target, and were expected to appear shortly after sun up. The engineer decided there was no point in moving. It would be much worse being caught on the ground. The main thing was to keep Vincent's bones out of reach. They could be an important bargaining chip although he had no intention of giving them up. Somehow he would get them to the government's office. But of course, Pistol Shot would have that well staked out. It was one problem after another. He decided to say

128

nothing to the others. There was no point in panicking them. At least they had the advantage of being high up. And Rocco would not fire indiscriminately for fear of hitting his prize.

The trees' new occupants found it difficult to settle. They feared nodding off and then falling off. Yet slowly voices became drowsy and silence finally descended. And Ibi was right. The only casualty was Andre who was severely winded when a vine broke as he tried to swing from one tree to the other. He had been unable to sleep and decided to go visiting.

He had just regained his place shortly after dawn when a shout came from below. The engineer edged along a limb and peered down. A familiar figure stood with his back to him, a grenade dangling from his belt.

"Keithy," it cried, as a host of startled birds took to the air. "Keithy, it's me, Rocco, your friend. We've come to thank you for the show. Now we want to entertain you. So come down." There was no answer. A hint of exasperation crept into his tone. "Are you coming down or not?" He fingered a gun in his pocket. "Keithy," he warned. "I know exactly where you are."

Silence is golden in such situations. Yet the engineer despite all his experience and commonsense, could not help himself. "Wrong tree," he shouted.

Pistol Shot spun round, a smile breaking over his brutal features. "So there you are. A very silly mistake. Now you can meet my troupe."

He raised a hand. A wave of armed men emerged from the undergrowth and surrounded the trees. The engineer was mortified. Duane next to him looked grave, but was secretly delighted. His friend was always calling him irresponsible and foolish. Well, who could talk now? He knew the English expression of putting your foot in it. This was a whole leg. Yet it was

129

everybody's legs. If Rocco saw one dangling from a branch he was likely to shoot it off. And Duane had no intention of being called Stumpy. He knew Pistol Shot well enough. Despite his sickly genial exterior, he would be boiling with rage inside. He had to be kept calm. His men's trigger fingers would be itching almost uncontrollably. One wrong word and the jungle would be ablaze.

"Humour him," he whispered to his companion.

That of course was easier said than done. Rocco was under as great a strain as Keith. He knew his followers were desperate to start the attack. Yet he knew one false move could spell disaster for Vincent The Knife's bones. That was the foreigners' trump card. And he was certain they were present. But had they put all their coconuts in one basket? Were they all in one tree? Or was the skull in one and the skeleton in another? He would need to find out.

His neck ached from constantly looking up. Things must be brought to a head. Normally he liked making puns, but this one was not funny. Not funny at all. "Keithy, you know why we are here. You have Vincent The Knife, yes?"

The engineer saw no reason to deny it. If he said he didn't, Rocco could attack immediately. He pictured bloodied bodies toppling off branches and crashing to the ground. Then being rolled over and having their wallets pinched. That was not the way to end their African adventure. Everybody had to be got home alive. But how? Things were beginning to look very tricky. Pistol Shot was still waiting for his answer.

"Yes, we have a skull and a skeleton." the engineer affirmed clearly. "We are handing them in to the government's office."

Rocco was equally clear. "No, Keithy, you are

handing them to me. Don't throw them down, lower them on a vine. We don't want anything broken."

"No," the figure above him repeated firmly. "We are the ones who will hand the remains in."

"So you are after the reward too eh?"

"It will go towards improving the life of the villagers."

Pistol Shot could not believe what he was hearing. What were better facilities for a bunch of country boys compared to beautiful chunky gold bracelets? The money would be in the wrong hands. He just managed to control his indignation. "But Vincent The Knife did not belong to your village. He was our leader, he belongs to the tenement."

"But you cannot hand him in. The police will know you are members of his gang. You will be arrested."

"And you cannot hand him in because you will be dead."

"Careful," Duane whispered to the engineer. "You're getting his blood up."

"Rocco, Rocco," Keith replied disarmingly. "There's no need to talk like that. We'll be happy to give you ten per cent."

"Ten percent?" Pistol Shot spluttered in disbelief. Split between the others, it would not buy him an earring - let alone a bracelet. There was angry muttering from his followers as they mentally downgraded their share.

The engineer sensed a tensing of an already fraught atmosphere. "All right, fifteen per cent," he declared quickly. This brought a snort of contempt from Rocco loudly echoed by his companions. Their leader fingered his grenade, beginning to wish it wasn't a dummy. Keithy could offer ninety percent but it would not be enough. Oh no, Vincent the Knife's motto had always been 'take the lot.' And that's what they would do. His memory had to honoured.

It was stalemate.

Rocco warned that if the remains were not lowered within five minutes, his men would start climbing. And if anybody trod on their fingers or poked them with a branch, they would be shot in self defence. The speaker stared ostentatiously at his watch hoping the threat would sink into the brains of those above. If they had any, they would immediately hand over the goods.

It was at moment that Lola arrived. She had discovered Duane's presence from the lookouts who had returned to the village in the early hours.

"My husband's in that tree," she cried.

Rocco's voice lacked any hint of pity. "We can make no exceptions. Everybody has to die."

"No, no, I want you to kill him."

Her listener looked incredulous. "You do?"

"He is a bad man, a naughty man, he ran off with another woman."

Pistol Shot relaxed. "A playboy eh?"

"He two timed me with a younger girl."

The gang leader just avoided a guffaw. What a card. Yes, he would spare him. The gang needed a joker. He peered upwards. "Which one is he? Can you see him? Try and point him out."

Duane, attempting to retreat further into the foliage, slipped. In grabbing a branch to save himself, he appeared in view. Lola's arm shot up. "There he is."

Rocco followed its direction and gasped in surprise. "Crusher, Cranium Crusher Jones."

The newcomer shook her head. "No, it's Duane."

"No, it's Crusher."

"No, no, it's Duane."

"No man, it's Crusher. He betrayed our gang."

Lola nodded. "Yes, that is him, a traitor."

Keith watching the animated scene, realised Duane was at last being useful. He had created a diversion. But how long would it last? Pistol Shot and Lola were quickly beginning to realise Duane and Cranium Crusher Jones were the same man. And there was no more talk of him being a card. Rather his card was being marked. His future was starting to look very bleak. Rocco wanted him shot instantly. He liked to see victims toppling from great heights. They made satisfying thuds as they hit the ground. Lola wanted him tied up first so she could give him a piece of her mind. In fact several pieces. Duane had endured such lectures for years and might then welcome a bullet behind the ear.

But before a decision could be made, a series of shots rang out. Rocco turned angrily on his men. Who had jumped the gun? No order to attack had been given. He was met with blank looks.

There was another burst of gunfire. A uniform figure stepped into view.

"Those were above your heads," the new arrival shouted. "If anybody moves the next volley will be at crotch level."

Captain Otis Yorke of the Lagos police was famed for his straight talking. And direct action. Other officers hit criminals where it hurts. He hit them where it hurt most. The gang stood like statues. Not a weapon wavered. They all knew this fearsome figure. The officer pointed to an open space near his feet. "Stack everything here."

A sheepish queue formed as one by one, they laid down their arms. Rocco appeared to have shrunk. He certainly felt like a pricked balloon. He was absolutely devastated. Yet he knew he could not sob in front of a

133

woman. Lola too, felt like bursting into tears. She knew her Duane. If she assaulted him now, he'd demand a police escort, citing domestic violence. Pistol Shot had no time for sympathy. Several deep furrows were creasing his brow. How had these latest visitors got here? Just as he was about to strike?

His friend Keithy of course could have told him. His call to inspector Howard had been followed by one from inspector Howard to captain Yorke. Captain Yorke had leapt from his chair, thrown the cigar he was chewing out of the window and hollered for his boys. He'd had his eye on Pistol Shot for a long time. Especially as Vincent the Knife appeared to be lying low. Just how low, he could never have imagined.

Rocco's motley crew found themselves outnumbered three to one. As Vincent The Knife used to say, such odds were sods. Pistol Shot knew he had to capitulate. Like all gangsters he loved a bloodbath as long as his own was not contributing to it. But it turned out to be a wise move. If the captain had concrete evidence of anything, he would have pounced earlier. So it had to involve any wrong doing taking place that day. What could the gang be charged with? Certainly not resisting arrest. They had behaved like lambs. He wracked his brains. Nothing. He felt a surge of confidence.

It was a subject also troubling the captain. He had been sure there would be a fight. The swift surrender posed a problem. There was no law against going armed into the jungle. And there was no proof the gang were going to shoot tourists out of trees. The indications might be there, but it would be hard to prove in court. Especially as the gang were all such liars and would never admit the truth.

The faces of their intended targets began to pop out

from their lofty perches. But nobody was climbing down. They wanted to know what was happening on the ground first. Their former besiegers were standing meekly in a group, watched closely by the armed officers who had emerged from the undergrowth. The captain was addressing a much more relaxed looking Rocco.

"So you city boys are having a day in the jungle?"

"That's right cap, we're on a picnic."

"Then why the fire power?"

"To shoot our lunch."

"What sort of game did you have in mind?"

Pistol Shot shrugged his shoulders. "Antelope, buffalo, whatever crosses our path."

"Nothing in human form?" The speaker pointed to the trees beside them.

Rocco gave a startled look, and nearly jumped out of his skin. "I never saw them man, What are they doing? Collecting nature's specimens?"

It was a wonderful theatrical effort but his companion was unimpressed. "There's only one specimen being collected today, and that's you."

Pistol Shot produced an air of injured innocence. "Cap, this is Rocco you are talking to. A man of peace."

"Then why are those people up there hiding from you?"

"Hiding from me, man? As I said, I've never seen them before."

His listener looked at Lola. "So you've got women in your gang now?"

" I'm not with them," she replied indignantly.

Rocco spread his arms wide. "Cap please, not gang - just a group of friends."

The officer felt enough was enough. Things were

going nowhere.

"Everybody empty your pockets," he commanded abruptly. Cigarettes were hurriedly stamped out as the order was obeyed. Other bits and pieces fluttered to the ground as the contents were displayed on open palms. The captain and two lieutenants carefully inspected them. There were no drugs. The gang leader watched confidently. He knew there was not. He had banned them on raids. He didn't want his own side carving each other up. "All clear eh?"

The officer ignored the question and nodded to his men. They stepped forward each producing a pair of shining handcuffs. These were snapped on still outstretched hands. The gang seemed to be in a collective shock. And none more so than Rocco who was shackled along with the rest.

"What's the charge man?" he almost shrieked. "What's the charge?" There was no reply. "You can't think of one, man can you? This is kidnapping, I'll sue you for wrongful arrest."

The captain pointed to the scattered dog ends and chewing gum wrappers. "Dropping litter," he said quietly.

Pistol Shot appeared to have difficulty believing his ears. "Dropping litter? There's no law in Nigeria against dropping litter."

Captain Otis Yorke remained unperturbed. "Maybe there is, maybe there isn't. We'll look at the statute book when we get to the station."

The prisoners were led away. A wave of relief swept through the watchers above. Not all the conversation had been audible, but the spectacle spoke for itself. They were saved! Keith was beside himself with delight. Not only had their besiegers been removed, they now had a police escort for taking in their prize.

136

He was about to begin his descent, when Frank appeared below. He gestured to the engineer to stay where he was. Despite his city attire, the newcomer scrambled up beside him. As he said, thank god he'd arrived in time. On no account was Keith to mention Vincent's bones to the police. Seeing his listener's incredulous look, he could only shake his head. Some Englishmen were not as intelligent as they should be.

"They'll want to share the reward," he explained. "And if they accompany you, they'll be entitled to it. Leave the remains in the tree and come back later. They'll be safe enough."

The engineer nodded. "That means we can then definitely have the reward all to ourselves?"

The lawyer shook his head once more. "Africa's not like that. You can hand in the skull, but will it be the one tested? It could be swapped. You could be given back someone else's and the officials would claim the money for the real one."

Keith sighed. "And there would be nothing we could do about it."

"No, but we must not let that happen."

"Easier said than done."

"Yes, you are learning."

On terra firma again, the party were profuse in their thanks to their rescuers. The captain looked quizzically at Keith. "Rocco doesn't normally rob foreigners. This isn't to do with that skull is it?"

The engineer shrugged. "You know that went missing from the cemetery some time ago." This was strictly true, and the speaker congratulated himself on not having told a lie. "Everybody's been looking for it," he added which was again a fact. The officer cast another dubious glance in his direction. He had a feeling this particular piece of bone would turn up at

137

the government office. And what a reward it would bring! It would not escape him. He would put a twenty four watch on the building with his best men.

The fugitives returned to the village for lunch before rebooking their hotel for what they hoped would be a final night. While tucking into a spicy stew, they discussed the two knotty problems facing them. First, they had to deliver the head to the authorities undetected. Keith had rightly judged from the captain's expression that he wanted a cut. If not the whole lot. He allowed himself a brief smile at the thought of the police and Rocco unknowingly conducting a joint operation. But it doubled the barrier they would have to get through. And once inside, they somehow had to avoid the skull being switched by unscrupulous officials.

There was as much scratching of heads as scraping of bowls. It was Sid of all people, who came up with the answer. "Chop it in half," he said.

"Chop what in half?" asked Joyce who was slow on the uptake.

"The skull. Keep half until the other half's been DNAd. Then we can send in the rest of the skeleton."

"Brilliant," said the vicar.

"Not really," replied the scheme's creator modestly. "It happens all the time in films when gangsters pay for a job. They cut bank notes in half and keep one lot until it's done."

"But how do we get our bit of head in?" asked Belinda who wished it had been decapitated a lot earlier. This brought a long silence. Getting past two sets of guards would be anything but child's play. Especially as neither would have any compunction over ruthlessly searching suspect visitors.

This time it was Trish who was struck with

138

inspiration. "A flower pot," she cried, jumping to her feet. "Fill one half with earth and stick a plant in it."

Ibi spoke for the first time. "That is good. Many people take gifts to the office. In England, I think you call them bribes. One of our youngest girls will take it. There will be no suspicion."

His remarks lifted a heavy cloud. The problems were solved! Admittedly the task still had to be carried out, but if the headman said it would work, then it would. All that had to be done now was collect the skull and skeleton from the tree and find the sharpest meat cleaver.

It was then the phone call came from Duane. Unable to climb down because of Lola waiting again with evil intent below, he had been left in charge of Vincent's remains. His message brought cries of dismay. A troop of monkeys had started to play catch with the skull. When he tried to intervene, they had run off with it. He had pleaded with Lola to follow them. She had reluctantly agreed after he promised he would stay where he was until she returned.

When the search party arrived at his tree, they could hear her voice. They hoped it meant the head was close. But Duane warned when aroused, his wife could be heard for miles. They plunged deeper into the jungle in search of their quarry. Soon the sound of excited chattering reached their ears. They entered a glade with an imposing tree in the centre. Underneath, an agitated Lola was peering up through the foliage. Above her, two of the thieves were lobbing the skull between them. A third was trying to intervene.

"Oh look," said Andre, "they're playing piggy in the middle." Silenced by a deadly glare from Keith, he decided to make amends. Helped by a handy shove, he began to climb the lower part of the trunk. But as he

139

went higher, so did the monkeys. Unnerved by the cries of encouragement from below, the holder of the skull tossed it high in the air. As the troop scampered off, it came to rest in the branch of an adjoining tree. This was at least thirty feet above the ground. There were no lower branches so climbing was out of the question. Every kind of missile within reach was hurled at the skull, but it could not be dislodged. It lay face down with its yellow teeth grinning at them. This became really annoying as the hours passed. Arms ached and aims became wilder. There were just two direct hits with coconuts, but they made no impression. The head was firmly wedged.

"There's nothing else for it," said Keith. "We'll have to cut the tree down."

Ibi regretfully shook his head. "We can't."

The engineer was astonished. "Why not?"

"We'll need a logging permit." He looked at the blank faces around him. "You can't cut anything down in the forest these days without a permit." He brightened. "But it should only take two or three weeks."

"I'm a grown man but I'm going to cry," declared Reggie. The mini bus in the long stay car park was looming again.

"Why can't we do it on the quiet?" asked Belinda. "There's nobody around here."

"You need a chain saw," replied Ibi. "That is a tell tale sound and would be heard a long way off."

"Then we'll have to use axes," said Keith. "If we get stuck in, it shouldn't take too long."

"Axes make a noise too." The head man was looking worried. He did not want to bring more trouble to his village.

"Think of the reward," said Andre. "Imagine Skulky

140

stuffed with notes."

"We can't leave him up there," warned the vicar. "He's behaved himself recently, but he could well take revenge."

"Talking won't get Vincent down," said Belinda impatiently. "We must do something now."

Ibi reluctantly, could see he had no option. He sent for his strongest men with orders to bring their axes. But after each strike they must attune their ears for approaching strangers.

"You can't chop and listen, chop and listen," said Andre. "We'll be here till doomsday."

Keith felt their own doomsday was fast approaching but knew for once the young chef was right.

It was then that Sid spoke up. "I've got another idea." Everybody stopped to listen. Especially after his astonishing earlier one. "We're under Lagos Airport's flight path. We could wait for planes to come over to drown the noise."

"We can't afford to hang around in between them," said Reggie irritably. "It's not Heathrow with one coming or going every minute."

"And what happens if the airport's closed because of fog?" cut in Andre.

"There's no fog in Nigeria," replied Trish. "Even I know that."

Ibi, who was wondering how Britain ever created an empire, took Keith aside. There were too many people around. They should wait at the village and the head would be delivered.

As the party returned to Duane's tree, Lola began peering up at it anxiously. She grudgingly gave him full marks for honesty. He was still there. Albeit several branches higher. He descended gingerly to his former level when he saw the group approaching. Safety in numbers.

The engineer explained what had happened to the skull. But he was fed up with having to shout to the fugitive or talk to him on his mobile. He was too useful to be stuck aloft with the crisis reaching boiling point. There was nothing else for it, he would have to become a marriage counsellor. He put a comforting arm round Lola. Would it help if he was to say sorry?

"If who was to say sorry?" she demanded.

"Duane."

Her eyes flashed. "He will not say sorry. He will be sorry. Very, very sorry." She glared up at the half hidden figure. "When he comes down I will show you."

"We don't want a bloodbath," called Andre.

Keith turned on him angrily. "You keep out of this." He addressed the rest of the onlookers. "Please return to the village and I will follow."

Duane was about to cry 'don't leave me,' but checked himself. He knew there had to be a showdown. Better to get it over and done with. And anyway, Paula had become too demanding. She was tiring him out. She had demanded what she called her 'smoochie smoo'' morning and night, but had now added lunchtime. At least with Lola, he'd got a decent rest. Well, apart from his ears. What if he did say sorry? What if he did ask to come home? One look at the indignant woman below told him he was dreaming.

Yet Keith was taking Lola by the arm. Many a kind and decent man had been led astray. They were as helpless as kittens in the hands of scheming, gold digging women.

Lola's brow knotted. "But we don't have any gold."

The engineer explained. A fast city girl plundering the pay packet of an innocent country boy. He knew this wasn't an exact picture of Duane, but it was the best he could do. But it had the wrong effect. The deserted wife frowned. All the things she wanted for her hut, Duane said he couldn't afford. Of course he couldn't. The money had gone on that bitch woman. She bent down to pick up a rock to hurl at the helpless kitten. Keith put his foot on it. "Lola, he still loves you!"

She stopped in mid stoop.

"It's true!" came the voice from above. "I want to come home."

The recipient of this news looked dazed.

"I really do." The tone floating down from above was increasingly urgent. "She's worn me out."

The engineer closed his eyes. No, Duane, no. That's not the approach. Yet Lola appeared not to hear. A fierce battle was going on inside her head. To forgive him? Or knife him? It could have gone either way when Keith tipped the balance. "Lola, you're too old to get anybody else. Better the devil you know."

The one in question, had come down to the lowest limb. He was still safely out of reach but close enough to work his special look. It had got him out of many scrapes. He conjured up a pair of dreamy pleading eyes above a soft half smile. Lola had fallen for it every time. It was his fatally bewitching gaze although the other women in the village thought it more a leer.

To Keith, it was a smug expression, and he feared Duane was already counting his chickens. Yet this time Lola was unmoved. She had regained her composure. If that man was coming back, he must pay.

"Come down here," she commanded. Duane's smile vanished and he looked uncertainly towards the engineer who had taken a big step backwards. He was a counsellor, he said. Not a referee. "You can't have a reconciliation from up there," he called.

143

The fugitive lowered a leg towards the ground as if testing the water. Would he be plunging into an icy sea? Or more likely, a molten volcano?

Lola stood like a statue. Duane inched his way down. His mouth was dry and he felt her eyes burning into his back. What was he to do first on the ground? That was the big question. He knew the answer. He turned with a dazzling smile, his arms outstretched in heartfelt welcome.

Lola's were already in action. Whack! She caught him across one cheek, and then the other.

"What's that for?" he cried. This brought a third, nearly knocking him sideways. Keith could only shake his head. 'What's that for?' Duane certainly had a way with words. The victim gingerly felt two tender patches forming either side of his half open mouth. The fatally bewitching gaze was nowhere to be seen. He sank to his knees. Lola took him by his collar and lifted him up. Just as she had many times after he'd been drinking whisky. The familiar ritual seemed to bring them closer.

"You bad, bad boy," she declared. Yet there was a slight softening of her tone. Duane, much to Keith's relief, said nothing. One wrong word could of set her off again. He kept a discreet distance as they walked slowly back to the village. He noticed with satisfaction, that the pair were holding hands. Yet on closer inspection, Lola's grip was vice like. Her returned husband would be going nowhere.

Chapter 24

The skull arrived at noon the following day. The tree had taken a lot of chopping, but the deed was done. The weary cutters, many still covered in sweat, put down their axes. They were joined by the English party who had returned earlier from their hotel. They sat in the shade on the edge of the clearing. The women came round with bowls of fruit. Executions should not be watched on an empty stomach. Not that it was a real one. Although to some, splitting a head in two seemed like it. One or two villagers preferred to stay in their huts.

The skull sat on a raised chopping block in the centre of the crowd. Scudding clouds cast fleeting shadows across it, giving the impression it was looking around.

"Skulky's making sure he knows who we are and where we live," said Andre. Nobody thought this funny. Especially his companions who remembered the bizarre events in England.

There was a discussion in hushed tones over what weapon to use. It was important for Vincent not to hear. Some opted for an axe with its greater swing. Others for a meat cleaver with its greater accuracy at close quarters. It was decided to let the chopper decide. But who was to be the chopper? Nobody had put themselves forward. Or intended to.

In the end the choice fell on Duane. After all, he had started the whole thing by taking Vincent's identity. He had been warmly welcomed back to the village, but several still thought it an awful cheek.

The executioner chose the axe. Swinging it over his shoulder with unerring aim, he brought it down with all his force. Whether it was the oohs of the crowd, or the rushing of the blade that caused the draught, will never be known. But the head toppled sideways just as the steel bit deep into the block. It lay on its side, its yellow teeth laughing at the onlookers.

"Did you see that," exclaimed Andre. "Skulky jumped out of the way."

"No, no it was the breeze," said the engineer. Surely that could be the only answer? He frowned. Or could it?

Ibi and Patu exchanged grave glances. The witch doctor had already been asked to mollify the skull with a spell but explained he lacked a relevant chant. A wave of near panic swept the crowd. Hadn't they told each other Vincent shouldn't be messed with? Now he would take his revenge.

Yet Duane remained calm. He placed two large stones either side of the head. It would take a hurricane to blow those over. Then he gave the target an icy stare. Keith, watching closely, felt his friend was imagining it to be either Paula's or Lola's. He could not decide which. This time the blade, flashing viciously in the sunlight, cleft the skull clean in two. There was a burst of spontaneous applause which quickly stopped. Nobody wanted to be seen celebrating. Vincent might be in two bits, but he could still be dangerous.

One half was sent for safety to the secret cave along with the skeleton which had been retrieved from the tree. The other was filled with earth and had an orchid planted in it. Now to find the courier. Etta was finally chosen. Not for being alert, quick witted or intelligent. The eleven year-old was slow, dim and unimaginative. She would not suffer nightmares because of her mission. There would be no vivid images of skulls and skeletons in her brain. She would just be carrying a bony flower pot to the government office. All she had to do was hand it in with an accompanying note after a journey of a hundred yards. She would be escorted to the corner of the street and given a gentle push in the right direction. Her normal vacant expression would take her sailing past the guards. The most astute detective or suspicious villain would never dream of stopping her.

There was a final debate over whether taking a finger from the skeleton would be easier. But as before, it was rejected. It was more impressive to leave the rest of the body intact. After all, the skull was the most important thing. Rewards were placed on the heads of bandits - not their feet or their elbows.

Three o'clock the next afternoon was to be zero hour. The double ring of watching guards should be nodding off after their lunch. Etta had not been to the city before. She was very excited. That is, she smiled slowly. Her mother would take her by bus. The flower pot would be hidden in a cardboard box for the ride. They didn't want other passengers peering at it.

Chapter 25

Captain Yorke sat across the table from Rocco whose handcuffs had been removed. They were in a side room at police headquarters. The atmosphere was not unfriendly.

"So why were you really in the forest?"

"I told you, for a picnic."

The officer sighed. "We'll forget the dropped litter, but I could connect you to fifteen robberies."

Pistol Shot laughed. "You need proof, cap."

His companion looked at him evenly. "There are ways and means of finding it."

The gang leader's face fell. "You wouldn't fit me up?"

The policeman shrugged. "We both know some are yours."

"That's the trouble with being famous - everything gets pinned on you."

"Infamous."

"Infamous, famous, whatever you like. We always have to carry the can."

The captain leaned forward. "There's no need to carry it."

Rocco frowned. "What do you mean?"

"You know there is a huge reward for finding Vincent the Knife, dead or alive?"

The prisoner nodded.

The speaker continued. "Of course you do. He is your main man." He paused meaningfully. "Or was."

Pistol Shot decided to hold his peace. He looked non-committally out of the window.

"That grave desecration we investigated," went on the officer. "There is an underworld rumour the remains did not belong to an innocent villager, but to a gangster."

Rocco was determined to give nothing away. "Well if they were, I don't know how they got there."

The captain nodded. "That of course is now immaterial. It is what happened to them afterwards that counts." He took the bull by the horns. "Look man, if my deductions are right, time is running out. You were in the jungle tracking down those foreigners. You did so because you know they have them. I have checked with the airport. The party have asked about return flights to England over the next three days. That means they are about to try to collect the reward. If we join forces we can prevent it and take the money for ourselves." His tone became increasingly urgent. "So tell me what you know."

Rocco swallowed hard. A picture of the gold bracelets flashed before his eyes. But could he trust the police? Of course not. The captain read his thoughts. "We could not split it fifty fifty," he admitted. "But as informants, you would get a hefty sum. "And," he paused, "there would be no need to tell all the gang would there?"

Pistol Shot pondered this in silence. The officer sensed he was weakening. "Everything will be done through official channels to guarantee your share. There will be no double crossing."

The gang leader heaved a big sigh. He knew he had to spill the beans, but the embarrassment of doing so turned him crimson. How could he admit a bunch of elderly tourists had stolen the skull from under his very nose? And from the depths of his headquarters? It didn't bear thinking about. Carefully he marshalled his words. They came out painfully and slowly. But he did not flinch from telling all. The only details omitted concerned Raymond's rearguard action on the john.

149

There were some things in life that needed a veil drawn over them.

When he had finished his sorry story, he expected his companion to utter a loud guffaw. But there was not even a snigger. In fact the officer felt moved enough to lean across and give the gangster's hand a sympathetic squeeze.

"The first thing you learn as a policeman," he said. "Is that appearances can be deceptive. They could well be a highly professional gang. We must be on our toes." He rubbed his chin thoughtfully. "The one called Porter. Maybe the woman sent him the head for safe keeping until the reward was announced."

Rocco was beginning to feel better. He had crossed swords with one of Britain's leading gangs. They had won the first round by a devious trick, but he would win the war. Or rather the reward. True, his new friend would have the lion's share, but together they would be unbeatable.

The captain brought him back to earth. There was no time for talking. The attempt to deliver the skull was imminent. But who would make it? Anyone from the English party would be too obvious. Being highly professional criminals, they would not take the risk. Nor could it be that traitor Cranium Crusher Jones. He too would be recognised immediately. That only left the villagers. Such a prize would never be trusted to a stranger. And what of them? It would not call for faint hearts, and many would be overawed by the big city. Yet the lure of a huge reward could stiffen their resolve. But how to recognise the carrier? There would be a bulky parcel for a start. Yet they had to be ready for all sorts of trickery. Anybody swathed in bandages for example, must be carefully prodded. There were devious minds at work. Of one thing the captain was sure. They would not use children. They could definitely be counted out. Rocco nodded sagely. It was comforting to have a razor sharp police mind on your side for once. The cap certainly knew his mangoes. He had privately thought they might use someone young and innocent. Now he could see how silly that was. Skulls were frightening things. They would terrify those of tender years.

Chapter 26

An expectant crowd assembled in the clearing as four o'clock neared. If the bus was on time, Etta and her mother would be returning any minute. It was only a short walk down the track from the stop. The pair had been given a quiet send off in the morning. It was important to keep everything normal. And those left behind tried to maintain the atmosphere all day. Yet the strain on their faces told a different story. Each was following the little girl in their mind. The bumpy bus journey, the nearing city, and the handover at the corner. Mamie taking the flower pot from its box and carefully checking the orchid. Then handing it to her daughter with last whispered instructions. The youthful figure walking slowly towards the hard faced guards with cold darting eyes which missed nothing.

At zero hour, every heart in the village beat in unison with Mamie's. Then it was the agonised wait for news. She disliked mobiles. An hour or two would make little difference. But it did. Every second seemed like an hour. Even the vicar, normally sanguine in such situations, tapped his watch to see if it had stopped.

At last the pair were approaching. Etta was skipping by her mother's side. This was seen as a good sign. But it raised false hopes. Mamie strode up to the onlookers and putting down her bag, extracted the split skull. It contained only clumps of earth. Everybody stared at it aghast.

Keith was the first to speak. "What happened?"

"It began good," said the chaperone. "Etta easy pass bad men. She reach steps of office when big, ugly man stop her. He pick orchid and put in buttonhole. Etta burst in tears. He fling coins at her feet. He hold flower pot while she pick up. Then he hand back. She run to

152

me. I cannot ask her go again."

The engineer closed his eyes and felt himself swaying. That description could only fit Rocco. Ibi too was mopping his brow.

It was Andre who summed up their thoughts. "Wow!" he exclaimed. "Lucky, lucky us. Pistol Shot nearly got Skulky."

Nobody disagreed with that. But what could they do now?

Chapter 27

The captain and Rocco were discussing the day's events. No attempt had been detected. There had been several fruitless searches. You couldn't be too careful. The man with the large box had been one. It was not their fault there were pigeons inside. Two had yet to come down from a nearby roof.

The meeting was taking place in the back of a dimly lit restaurant near the government office. The pair valued their quiet seclusion but it did not last. Raymond burst in excitedly. He had to be told twice to keep his voice down. He'd been buying sweet potatoes from a voluble villager.

"They are using a child," he cried. "A child with a flower."

The captain gave a surprised frown. "When?"

"Any time now."

The officer turned shamefacedly to Pistol Shot. "Man, I owe you a big apology. I was certain they would not use kids."

"Think nothing of it," replied Rocco who suddenly seemed far away. He was looking at his hands as if wishing to chop them off. He had held the precious skull! Well, half of it. All he had to do was walk up the steps and hand it in. Yet he'd passed it back to that blubbering girl. A moment of weakness! A moment of compassion! That's all it had taken. If his legs weren't under the table, he would have kicked himself. Vincent The Knife certainly would have. Probably in the crotch. And he would have deserved it. What had his old boss said? Never show mercy. Never have a kind thought. Once again he'd failed to learn a lesson. He vaguely heard his companion saying 'sorry' again.

He pulled himself together. "Now cap, don't take it

to heart. We all make mistakes."

He did not feel it was the right moment to reveal his own. It would not be fair to upset his new friend further. At times you had to think of others despite what Vincent The Knife said. But looking on the bright side, at least she had run off without delivering it. He would not be so foolish next time.

But the officer was quickly recovering his composure. He addressed Raymond with his old authority. "Do we have any more details?"

"Why yes," came the reply. "The flower is an orchid." He looked at Rocco's jacket slung over the back of his chair. "Like the one in the buttonhole."

"They're very popular," the gangster responded hurriedly. "You can get them anywhere in the market." Sweating profusely, he congratulated himself on his swift reply.

However the captain's mind was moving on. "It could be a decoy."

"What could?" said Rocco.

"The flower."

"Yes, yes it could be," replied his companion with great relief. "I know those villagers. They're all liars."

"We must be extra alert. I will put an officer on the top step."

"And I will put Puncher John on the bottom one."

The captain nodded. "There will be no way through."

"Yes, we'll take it off them on the threshold. Then we won't have to carry it far."

Raymond was sent for two large rums to toast the inevitable triumph.

Chapter 28

A large black cloud hung over the village blocking out the sun. It was as if nature was plunging it deeper into gloom. Even the flies were subdued. Intense thinking was causing headaches. How could the skull now be delivered? Nobody had any idea. It looked an impossible task.

The English party were becoming restless. It was not a case of enough was enough, said Reggie, but of enough was enough, was enough. First they had stayed until one thing happened. And then until something else happened. Now it was just another twenty four hours which no doubt would become forty eight hours or even longer. He was worried about his pub and the vicar about his church. And Trish was fretting over her seagull. None of the party could deliver the head because as foreigners they would stand out. There was nothing more they could do.

Keith had to agree. It was time to go home. But could they leave the village in the lurch at the last hurdle? The landlord said he was fed up with last hurdles. They kept cropping up all the time. The engineer discreetly sought out the others to find they agreed. Even the loyal Belinda was for it. She had chosen her top ten ways of getting rid of Vincent, from hurling him over a cliff to carving him into ashtrays. This would add great pleasure to stubbing out cigarettes.

A flight was available the following day. Everybody was booked on it except for Keith. He felt he had a duty to stay until the bitter end.

A farewell dinner was organised. But nobody felt like drinking or dancing. The only sound among the fireflies was the scraping of bowls. They were like monks in a monastery. It was then that Sid leapt into the air. "Post it!"

"Post what?" said Joyce.

"The skull, post the skull! They'll never search the mailman. They'd never think we'd let it out of our sight."

There was a startled murmur. The speaker felt all eyes on him. Keith pinched himself and then Sid who shouted "ow!" No, what the engineer had heard was real.

"What did you do that for?" cried the afflicted figure, rubbing his arm. But Keith could only stare at him in wonder. A ridiculously simple solution had been staring them in the face. And who had seen it? Only Sid. He couldn't take it in. What about the vicar? Or Reggie? Or himself? They called themselves the brains trust. The heart of the pub quiz team while Sid was relegated to handing round the cheese and onion sandwiches. Well, they would change that. His name would be first on the list from now on. Keith shook his head in admiration. And who had suggested chopping the skull in two? Why Sid of course. They again had been left far behind.

The others were echoing his thoughts. They gazed at their saviour with a mixture of awe and gratitude. Sid, who was still on his feet, puffed out his chest and went round shaking hands. It was preferable to being slapped on the back because his dentures were none too secure.

"Don't strut," called Joyce irritably. But the flamboyant figure felt he had every right to. Where had the idea come from? He had no idea. It had just popped into his head. When these did, he used to study them before speaking. But then they popped out again and he forgot what they were. So now he spoke out immediately which had caused the electrifying effect.

A vibrant buzz took over. Some of the party wished they were not going home tomorrow but knew they had to. Otherwise they were in danger of going native. Tom was worried that Rita had taken up chewing betel nuts.

The coach stood waiting to take the guests back to their hotel for the last time. There were hugs and kisses and not a few tears as the villagers said goodbye. The English party were upset they would miss celebrating the reward, if indeed it was collected. But in truth they were danced out. Reggie for one, was looking forward to a pint. The local brew had made his nose bleed. The vicar regretted he had not made any conversions. Yet he had taught two verses of Onward Christian Soldiers to several youths. Although he admitted these did not sound the same when chanted. Trish had turned down two marriage proposals. The second while dancing 'The Shimmy'. She hastily dropped it from her routine but was not sorry. It was difficult making the tassels go in different directions. Andre had picked up new ingredients for his shepherd's pie. Reggie had OK'd these as long as the chef tried them out on himself first.

At last they crowded into the bus. Keith went too. He would go to the airport to see them off. And on the way post the parcel by recorded delivery. It was packed in thick paper with strong twine. It would not encourage casual opening.

And so it was that Sid was proved right. The watchers on the office steps waved on the delivery boy. And Puncher in a moment of benevolence, opened the door for him.

Chapter 29

Keith and Duane sat under their favourite tree sipping whisky. The reward had been verified and a few loose ends tidied up. The engineer knew that despite its riches, the village would suffer if the police and Rocco remained its enemies. So he had prevailed upon Ibi to make a donation to police funds. This had allowed the captain to buy a new fridge and television and take his wife on holiday. The gangster was looked after too. After all, they had stolen Vincent's skull. Keith met him as arranged, outside a city centre jewellers. The money was torn from his fingers. The next minute two chunky gold bracelets were being delightedly swung in the air.

With everything sorted out, the engineer was departing in the morning. He looked up at the stars. He had come full circle. He would definitely not be going round again. Duane had taken a large swig and was holding him by the arm. "What fun eh man? What a laugh." He gave his lips a wipe with the back of his free hand. "You and me together eh? We have adventures."

Keith kept his voice calm. "Not any more."

His friend wriggled a finger in his ear as if he hadn't heard properly. "What you say?"

"Not any more," Keith repeated firmly. "Belinda and I will be setting out alone in the next world."

Duane had tears in his eyes. "What about me?"

"Lola will keep an eye on you."

"No, she will post me. Put me in a corner of your tomb. I will be a good boy."

The engineer pictured the scene and shuddered. He patted his friend on the shoulder. "Remember the last time? You will forget all this in the morning."

Duane shook his head doggedly. "No, no, this time

159

it's serious. We won't be together in the next world if we don't stay together."

Keith nodded. "Exactly."

His companion peered at him in the darkness. "Exactly what?"

"Exactly that. Nothing will happen." He got to his feet, swaying slightly. "It is kind of you to offer to accompany me, but the answer is no."

The speaker set off unsteadily for Lola's hut with one thing on his mind. He must warn Belinda never again to sign for a strange parcel.

The End